EAGLE DOWN

RICHARD FLETCHER

Copyright © 2017 Richard Fletcher
All rights reserved
First Edition

PAGE PUBLISHING, INC.
New York, NY

First originally published by Page Publishing, Inc. 2017

ISBN 978-1-63568-381-3 (Paperback)
ISBN 978-1-63568-382-0 (Digital)

Printed in the United States of America

CHAPTER 1

Georgetown is a small community in Washington, DC, just north of the Francis Scott Key Bridge, carrying traffic from Arlington, Virginia, to Washington, DC. It is an upscale community in which many government politicians live. It's convenient for employees and officials to the capital and other federal government offices.

On this day, it was a warm night in July. The temperature had been in the low nineties that day. The sun was down, and most all people were already in bed, sleeping. The issues of the day were put on hold until sunrise the following day, when debates would rage under the Capitol rotunda as the Senate and House of Representatives debated a series of new bills requested by the new president. There was only a quarter moon that night, giving little light to the town. It was one o'clock in the morning. All was quiet. Even the birds, which had been chirping all day, were quietly resting in the branches of the trees. During the day, the bridge was extremely busy since it was the main thoroughfare between Virginia and Washington, DC, but vehicle traffic at that hour was minimal; barely a car could be seen traveling the streets.

A black Mercedes sedan drove slowly up a street in Georgetown. A man was the only occupant of the car, and he was looking for an address. He was a sinister-looking individual. His hair was jet-black and came to a widow's peak over his forehead. He wore a thin black mustache and a well-groomed goatee. He was thin and tall, just over six feet. He was wearing a black turtleneck sweater, a black coat over his turtleneck sweater, and black pants and shoes. On his hands, he wore latex gloves. As he drove along, he spotted the house he was trying to locate. He looked at a notepad to be sure it was the correct address. The house was in an upscale neighborhood and designed using typical Georgian architecture. When he assured himself that it was the correct address, he continued down the block for several hundred feet and parked his car on the opposite side of the street. He sat for a few minutes, making sure no cars were coming and no pedestrians were walking their dogs or out exercising. When he was sure he was totally alone, he got out of the car and briskly walked back to the house. On the stone stoop, he bent over and located the lock on the front door then took a small tool out of his pocket, inserted it into the keyhole, and jiggled it. Then he quietly turned the doorknob, and the door opened.

He quickly slipped inside the house, closing the door quietly behind him. The house was dark, with only a small amount of moonlight coming through the windows, making it difficult to see. He was not familiar with the layout of the rooms, so he had to move slowly, feeling his way. He came to the stairs that led up to the upstairs bedrooms on the second floor. Slowly he climbed the stairs one by one, making sure no stair made a squeaking noise under his foot. When he reached the top of the stairs, he saw four doors. He went to the first door and quietly turned the doorknob. He opened it slowly. The moonlight shone on the bed, and he could see it was unoccupied. He closed the door and went to the next door. It was partially ajar. Looking in, he could see it was a bathroom. Farther down the hall, he came to another door. Again, he quietly turned the doorknob and opened the door quietly. He looked in and saw a single figure in a single bed. He closed the door and went to the last door in the hallway. He hesitated for a moment then reached behind his back and took out a Beretta automatic with a long silencer on the muzzle from his waistband. He turned the doorknob and quietly opened the door. He saw two figures in bed, sleeping. He tiptoed to the left side of the bed, looking closely to make sure the figure was a man. Satisfied it was a man, he put the Beretta to the back of the man's head and pulled the trigger. As the bullet entered the man's head, his body jerked and rose slightly and came down to rest. The muffled noise of the Beretta with the silencer barely stirred the woman on the other side of the bed. She let out a soft moan and moved ever so slightly.

The assailant moved around the bed, aimed the Beretta at her head, and pulled the trigger. Other than a slight jerk, she barely moved. The assailant put his hand on the carotid artery of the woman and picked up the empty brass shell ejected by the gun. Then he went around to the man, checked his artery, and picked up the other brass shell. Satisfied they both were dead, he left the room, closed the bedroom door, quietly went down the stairs, and left the house, closing the front door behind him, making sure it was locked. When he got in his car, he took out his cell phone and dialed a number. It rang several times. When someone answered, he said, "It's done." He closed the lid on his phone then drove away into the night.

* * *

Sitting at her desk in the newsroom of the paper the *Washington Ledger*, Carol Williams was putting the final touches on a story she had just finished writing. The deadline for turning in the story was later in the day, for it to make the deadline for the afternoon edition, and it was only eight o'clock in the morning. Carol was a reporter for the *Washington Ledger*, a newspaper in Washington, DC. She had been with the newspaper for seven years. She first joined the paper after graduating from college, majoring in journalism. Her goal in life was to have a byline on a major newspaper. When she first joined the paper, she was made the roving reporter, interviewing people on the street about topics of the day, which she detested. But she realized the only way to get into the newspaper business was to take any job that was offered and to work one's way up the ladder. After several years, she was assigned to a desk in the newsroom, handling minor stories. Just a year ago, she was assigned to the police beat, covering crimes, including murder.

Carol could be considered an attractive woman. She had a nice figure and a very pleasant face and spoke softly. She didn't date much because her first priority was her job; social life came afterward. Her job left little time for any romance. She always got to the office before eight each morning and viewed the police reports for anything that would be on her beat. Carol was still trying to get over the terrible, uneasy feeling she had covering murders. Her newspaper partner, Bob, had assured her that in time, she would get used to it.

Sitting at a desk across her was her partner, Bob Grant. He had been with the paper longer than Carol and was teaching her the ways of a good newspaperwoman. At thirty-nine years old, Bob was a fairly good-looking man. He was reasonably tall, just under six feet, with blond hair and blue eyes, and he still had his muscular physique. He had been in the army for two years, which helped pay for his college education. He had been on the police beat for four years and was acquainted with all the detectives in the homicide division.

He watched Carol type the final sentence to her story in her computer and sit back to read it.

"Finished?" he asked.

She looked up, nodded, and said, "Yep!"

"How about joining me for a cup of coffee in the cafeteria?"

"Sure, why not?"

As they got up to leave, Bob saw Sam Corcoran through the big glass windows to his office franticly waving his arms for them to come inside. Sam's office was all glass on the front, facing the newsroom. Bob said, "The chief wants us."

Carol looked and saw Sam waving his hands to come in. When they got there, they saw Sam watching the television screen in his office. Bob asked, "What's up, Chief?"

Sam said nothing and pointed to the television screen. On the screen was a woman reporter holding a microphone. They both caught the name Harry Bigelow, which piqued their interest. Harry Bigelow was the assistant to the chief of staff of the president of the United States. The reporter went on to say Bigelow and his wife, Dorothy, were found dead by their fifteen-year-old daughter, Caroline, this morning. The police said it was a double homicide.

Sam turned the television off.

"Okay, you two get on this story right away. Jesus Christ, a man in the office of the president murdered! What a story."

"Where does he live?" asked Bob.

"Here, I wrote it down," he said, handing Bob a piece of paper. "In Georgetown."

Sam Corcoran was the editor of the paper. Although he was in his fifties, he still had a good head of hair, which was beginning to gray. He wore dark-rimmed glasses with bifocals. He was of average height and wore suspenders and a belt, which indicated to most that he didn't trust the suspenders. Sam had been in the newspaper business since he was nineteen. His first job was as copyboy. He came up to his current position the hard way. He was a hard-driving editor who demanded confirmation on any story.

Bob and Carol left the office, went to the parking garage, and drove to Georgetown, to the Bigelow residence. Outside the house were many police cruisers and a paramedic's van, all with their colored lights still flashing, giving the area a psychedelic, dance hall feeling. Near the front entrance to the house was a woman reporter with one of the major television networks. She had a microphone up to her mouth, and a television cameraman was taking her picture as she spoke.

Looking around, Bob saw a policeman he knew. He went over to him and asked, "Hi, Gerald. What's going on?"

"Hi, Bob. A bigwig, a fellow by the name of Harry Bigelow, and his wife were murdered last night. Their daughter found them in their bed this morning."

"A bigwig, I'll say. He worked in the president's office. How were they killed?"

The detective replied, "Shot in the head."

"Who's on the case?"

"Detective Terry Branigan. Know him?"

Bob said, "Yeah. We've worked with him before. Anything else?"

"I haven't been in the house, so all I know is what the sergeant told me," Gerald said.

"Thanks. Carol, let's see if Dorothy, the TV broadcaster, has anything more."

They went over to Dorothy, who was just finishing her broadcast. He heard her say "Cut" and then went up to her.

"Hi, Dorothy. What have you got? I understand from your broadcast that there were two victims who were shot and the daughter found them this morning in their bedroom. Anything else?"

"No, Bob. I've been going over his résumé as a fill-in, but what you have heard is all the police have told us."

They waited around, talking to the news camera crew and policemen, until Detective Branigan came out. Then all the newspeople rushed over to ask questions from Branigan, Bob and Carol included.

Branigan stopped on the stone stoop as the reporters rushed toward him. "Ladies and gentlemen," Branigan began, "I really don't have anything new for you. At this time, all we have is that Mr. and Mrs. Bigelow were murdered sometime last night. The assailant used a pistol and shot them in the head. We have no leads, no time of death. We will have to wait until the medical examiner completes his autopsy before we can establish anything more. The crime scene investigators are in the crime scene now, combing for evidence. That's all I have for now!"

He pushed his way through the crowd of reporters while they shouted questions at him. He got in his cruiser and left. Shortly afterward, attendants in white uniforms pushed two gurneys out of the house with the bodies of the victims and put them in the medical examiner's van.

Bob said to Carol, "Let's get back to the office and see what we can dig up on him from our morgue files."

* * *

Gerald Harrison was the president of the United States. He had been elected the previous November and inaugurated in January. It had been a bitter campaign between the two parties. The country was in a severe recession. Unemployment was at an all-time high, and the economy was at its worst since the Great Depression in the 1930s. Retail sales were at their lowest since the end of World War II. The population was demanding that something be done. Each candidate promised to bring the country out of the recession, and Harrison promised to spend enough money to bring the country out of the recession by creating jobs in the private sector and the government sector. He had chosen a woman, Grace Arden, as his running mate.

She was a two-term governor, had eight years experience as an executive running a state, and had brought her state from one in deficit to one in a balanced budget—a good fit for Gerald Harrison's platform. His opponent took an opposite view by promising to reduce taxes for everyone, including small and large business. In the end, Harrison won by a small majority of the votes.

In the first months of his administration, he put together a spending package of one and a half trillion dollars. The House of Representatives and the Senate were having a bitter debate over the bill. The debate reached radio talk shows, all the newspapers in editorials, and even the major networks on the evening news. Harrison had been on television a number of times, pushing his bill. Polls taken from time to time showed the people were only 52 percent behind their new president. Grace Arden, the vice president, was out traveling around the country, holding rallies for the president's plan. She was very popular.

This morning, Harrison was having breakfast and reading the newspaper. He always had all the major newspapers delivered to the White House each day. He would read all the editorial pages to see which way the debate was going. He had just completed his breakfast when a butler came in and told him his chief of staff, Paul Barrows, had to see him. It was urgent.

"Okay, Henry, have him go to the oval office. I'll be down in a minute."

When Harrison walked into the oval office, Paul was sitting on the sofa.

The president said, "Good morning, Paul. What's so urgent? Do we have another terrorist attack?"

"No, Mr. President. Something very close to home."

"Oh? What's that?"

Paul Barrows hesitated then said, "Harry Bigelow was murdered last night."

"*What?* You mean your assistant?"

"Yes, sir. Both he and his wife."

"Who did it? Do the police have a suspect?"

"No. From what I got from the chief of police, he and his wife were shot with a small handgun with a silencer. When they didn't come down for breakfast, their fifteen-year-old daughter went up to their bedroom, found them, and called 911. So far, they have no leads, and the autopsy will tell them the caliber of the gun. There were no shell casings. The assailant must have picked them up."

"How did he get in?"

"Can't tell. The chief said there was no break-in. The assailant must have had a key or knew how to jimmy the lock."

"Was it a robbery gone bad?" the president asked.

"The chief didn't think so. The daughter said she couldn't see anything missing. The chief said, from the position of the bodies in the bed, they were asleep when they were shot."

"What would be the motive to kill that man?"

"I don't know. From what I knew of Harry, he was a well-respected family man. I never got any hint he might be having an affair or have had any kind of a drinking or gambling problem. He was squeaky clean. I looked at the FBI report I had done on him before I hired him. There was nothing out of the ordinary."

"What could be the motive to kill him and his wife? I'm going to call Clive Banner. I'll get the FBI in on this."

"Do you want me to call him?"

"Yes, Paul. Get him over here right away."

* * *

Bob was sitting at his desk when Carol came into the newsroom. She walked over to her desk, threw her notebook on it, and sat in her chair. She put her folded hands on her lap and looked down, exasperated.

Bob looked over at her and saw she was dejected. "What's wrong, Carol? You look like you lost your best friend."

"I spent three hours going through the files, looking for something on Bigelow. Nothing. Absolutely nothing. All I got was he graduated from Yale, went to law school, worked for a law firm in New York, then went to work for Harrison's campaign. Other than getting married and having two kids, he never even had a traffic ticket. He's clean."

"I wonder why he was murdered," Bob lamented.

"That's a job for homicide. Did you call Branigan?"

"Yeah. But he gave me nothing."

"Well, we'll have to run the story mostly with a résumé on his career and ask the question, 'Why was he killed?' Let's go talk to the chief."

They got up and went into Sam's office. When they stood in front of his desk, he asked, "What have you got?"

"Other than what the newscast says on TV, nothing," said Bob.

"Nothing? Have you gone through the morgue downstairs?"

"Yes, sir," said Carol. "I spent three hours and didn't find a thing other than his résumé and marriage."

"Damn it, dig! The assistant chief of staff to the president of the United States doesn't get murdered for no reason. Do you have any contacts in the White House?"

"No, sir, but I have a contact in the FBI."

"Well, squeeze him. I'll bet the FBI will be in on this. For Christ's sake, we're talking about the highest government office in the land."

* * *

Clive Banner, the director of the FBI, walked into the oval office. "Good afternoon, Mr. President," he said.

"Hello, Clive. Sit down."

As he sat on the couch, he asked, "What's on your mind, Mr. President?"

"No doubt you have heard that Harry Bigelow was murdered last night along with his wife."

"Yes, I heard. I'm sorry. I understand he was well liked here."

"I understand the Washington police have no leads on the killer. Harry was an upstanding husband and father. Paul, my chief of staff, went through his resume and looked at the report your department made at his request before hiring him. He found nothing. Absolutely nothing. I want your department to take charge of the investigation. I want to get to the bottom of this."

"Yes, of course we can. I'll get a team on it right away. I'll put my best agent, Dan Morris, on it. But you do realize that we will have to look in your house and talk to all the personnel in the White House. We will have to take his computer and see if anything shows up there."

The president responded, "Do what you need to do but get to the bottom of this."

"Fine. I'll get my crime scene men over to the house and see if they can come up with something."

As Clive got up to leave, the president grabbed his arm. "Clive, keep me posted on this. This is personal."

Clive smiled and responded, "Yes, sir."

* * *

Later that afternoon, a team of FBI agents descended on the White House. Special Agent Dan Morris was heading the team. He joined the Federal Bureau of Investigation as soon as he graduated from law school and worked his way up in the bureau for ten years. And Clive Banner considered him his best agent. Dan was approaching his thirty-ninth birthday, but he had maintained his physique by going to the gym whenever he could. He was a good figure of a man, good-looking and tall, and he still had the glimmer of a baby face.

Dan and the other agents began questioning everyone who had any contact with Harry Bigelow. They took his computer back to the forensic lab to search the hard drive for anything unusual. After they had gone through the files, all they found was an e-mail that Bigelow had sent to George Saxton, the majority leader in the Senate, and a copy to Vice Admiral Benjamin Goodman, head of the National Security Agency.

> *I have heard of something called Eagle Down from one of your assistants. After he mentioned it, he said it concerned national security and he couldn't*

talk about it. Can you enlighten me what this program is? I don't think Paul Barrows knows anything about it.

The forensic lab sent this to Clive Banner, and he read the memo. Dan was in Clive's office. He pondered for a moment then handed the memo to Dan. "What do you make of this?"

Dan read the memo. "I have never heard of any bill or program called Eagle Down."

"I haven't either. I think I'll talk to George Saxton. If it's a bill or some new program, the senate majority leader will know something about it. Send this to all the agents working the Bigelow case. Tell them to let me know if they hear anything connected to this Eagle Down."

* * *

The next morning, Clive was sitting in the majority leader's office.

"Tell me, Clive, what can I do for the FBI today?"

"The president has asked me to investigate the Bigelow murder."

"Oh? How come? Isn't that a DC police matter?"

"Yes, but since Bigelow is in the president's office, he took it personally and asked me to investigate."

"So how can I help you?"

"In going through Bigelow's computer, we came across an e-mail that Bigelow sent you and the national security chief, asking about a program called Eagle Down."

"Yes, I recall that. I wondered who on my staff could have told him that. I have never heard of that before. I was going to call him, but of course, he's dead, so now it's a moot point."

"So you never heard of this Eagle Down?"

"No. If had, I would tell you."

"Do you mind if I talk to all your assistants?"

"No, of course not. But I can tell you, if I haven't ever heard of this Eagle Down, none of them have."

"Fine. I'll send one of my agents over tomorrow to talk to them."

* * *

The next morning, Dan Morris was in the office of George Saxton. He questioned each one of his people, but no one had ever heard of Eagle Down. He reported the results of his questioning back to Clive Banner, so Banner dropped the matter as a nonevent.

That afternoon, the *Washington Ledger* hit the streets. The front-page story was the Bigelow murder. The story carried pictures of Harry Bigelow and his wife. All other news was a repeat of his college career, his working for a law firm, and his job working for the president's campaign.

After the paper hit the streets, Sam Corcoran called Carol and Bob into his office. "Okay, you two, what new items on the Bigelow murder have you got?"

"Nothing new, Chief. The autopsy is done. The police said the time of death was around one o'clock and the bullets were from a nine-millimeter pistol. That's it," Bob said.

"Did crime scene investigators find anything?"

"If they did, they are keeping it to themselves."

Sam asked, "Didn't you say the FBI is on the case?"

"Yes. That's what we were told."

Sam turned to Carol and asked, "Carol, don't you have a friend in the FBI?"

"Yes. Dan Morris. I used to date him," she responded.

"Well, get in touch with him. See if the FBI has uncovered anything."

"Okay, but he may not want to talk about the case."

"Use your womanly wiles on him. Promise him something. But get him to talk," Sam demanded.

"Are you suggesting I sleep with him?"

"Well, didn't you when you were dating him?"

Slightly embarrassed, Carol said, "That, *sir*, is none of your business."

"Okay, but get something out of him. Now get out of here and get me something to print."

They left his office and went back to their desks. Neither of them spoke for a minute. Then Bob said, "Well, are you going to call him?'

"Yes, but I haven't spoken to him for a while. He'll know for sure I want something, and if we have dinner, he will expect me to go to his apartment."

"Well, tell him straight out that you want to talk about the Bigelow murder. That way, you are under no obligation, just dinner."

"I guess. Okay, I'll call him."

Carol looked up the FBI phone number and got an operator. Then Dan came on the phone. "Hello? Agent Morris here."

"Hello, Dan. Carol Williams here."

"Carol! I haven't heard from you in over a year. What are you up to now? Still with the *Washington Ledger*?"

"Yes, Dan, and I'm working on the Bigelow murders. I understand the bureau is involved in the investigation."

"Yes. As a matter of fact, I'm working on the case along with several other agents."

"Can we have dinner tonight?"

Dan responded, "Sure, but, Carol, you know I can't divulge any information to the newspaper."

"I know, but I would like to talk to someone on the investigation to make sure we have our facts straight. Nothing more."

"Okay. Why don't we meet at Oscar's? You always liked that place. Say, at seven?"

"Seven it is. See you tonight."

She hung up and sat there for a moment, then she said to Bob, "I've got a dinner date tonight at seven. But he said he can't divulge any information on the case."

"Well, maybe if you turned on your charm, he might slip and say something."

"I don't know. Dan's a careful man. His whole life is the FBI," Carol responded.

"Carol, we know the FBI has had a forensic team at the Bigelow's and has gone over that whole house. Surely, they've found something. A guy just doesn't walk into a house, go upstairs, shoot two people, and leave without leaving something behind."

"The DC police didn't find anything."

"Yeah, but the FBI has a much better team and lab than the police," Bob said.

The rest of the day, they went about researching another murder of a homeless man. That evening, Carol picked out her best dress and spent a lot of time on her makeup. She wanted to mesmerize Dan and keep him off his guard so he would say something about the Bigelow murder. At six forty-five, she got in her car and drove to Oscar's in Falls Church, where she lived. The parking attendant parked her car. When she walked in, the maître d' showed her to a table. Dan was already there. He got up and pulled the chair out for her.

"Carol, you look beautiful. I'd forgotten what a beautiful woman you are," Dan said.

"Thank you, Dan. That's kind of you."

Not beating around the bush, he said, "Let me ask you straight out. Is there any chance of us picking up where we left off?"

"My, you are direct. No, I don't think so. You are dedicated to your job, and so am I. That's the reason we broke up before. I can't see that anything has changed."

"Well, you can't blame a guy for trying, as the saying goes."

"No, I guess not."

"Let's cut through the BS. Why did you want to have dinner with me? I told you I can't divulge anything the FBI has discovered in the Bigelow murders."

"I know. But I would like to go over the case and see if I have everything that has been made public."

"Okay, shoot. Let's see what you know," Dan said.

"The medical examiner's report says that the two were shot with a weapon that uses a nine-millimeter shell, probably a Beretta."

"Correct so far."

"He also said the killer murdered them at around one o'clock."

"Correct again."

"The police said there were no shells found at the scene. The murderer picked them up, and the murderer didn't break into the house. He either had a key or he picked the lock. When the police arrived, the front door was still locked."

"Right on target."

"If he had a key, that means he knew the Bigelows. Have you or the police looked at all the acquaintances of the Bigelows?"

"We have talked to a number of them. Most had an alibi for the time of death of the Bigelows. You know, the married partners were in bed. Some were out of town. They had a large array of friends. We haven't talked to all of them, but we checked to see if they had a license for a gun. So far, no leads."

Carol asked, "How about the White House?"

"Nothing there."

"There's a lot of fighting going on over the president's bill. Could that play a part here?"

"I doubt it. He is just an assistant to the chief of staff. He played no part in designing the bill," Dan said.

"There must be something. Very few murders are perfect crimes."

"True. We looked at his background, talked to former classmates and business partners, and got no leads. I'm waiting for the final results of the forensic team to see if anything shows up there. We had them go through his computer to see if that would yield something. The only thing that seems out of the ordinary is a reference to something called Eagle Down."

"Eagle Down?" Carol asked, her interest piqued.

"Yeah. It was in an e-mail he sent to the majority leader in the Senate and the director of national security. Both of them said they have no idea what Bigelow was talking about. They never heard of a bill or program with that name."

"When did he send the e-mail?"

"The day before he was murdered."

"Could that have something to do with his murder?"

"We found no connection to that since no one seems to know anything about a program or bill by that name. Probably someone gave Bigelow wrong information or was just pulling his leg. Besides, why would his wife be murdered for something Bigelow did?"

Slightly exasperated, Carol asked, "Then you have no new clues or leads?"

"Like I said, if forensics doesn't come up with anything from the crime scene, we are back to square one."

"Tell me, is it possible the murderer came in a window and left footprints?"

"No. We checked every window and examined all the ground in front of the windows. No. He came in the door. How, we don't know. I'm sorry I can't give you anything more, and if I had more, I couldn't divulge it to you."

"Okay, Dan, let's order."

When Carol was driving home, the phrase "Eagle Down" kept running through her mind. Was it a reference to the eagle preservation to increase the eagle population? Or maybe the symbol on coins and the national seal, which displayed an eagle? And what would that have to do with a murder of two people? Baffling!

* * *

The next morning, Paul Barrows was in the president's office, discussing the debate in the Senate of his stimulus bill. He said, "Mr. President, so far, it looks like we don't have enough votes to pass your bill. I spoke with the speaker of the House, and he says you should bring the muscle of the White House to bear on some of the no votes. I'm sure we can find a few representatives that want something for their district."

"You mean bribe them?" shocked, the president asked.

"Yes. It's been done by every administration since Roosevelt. It's legitimate. I can get a list of names from the speaker of the House and have him find out what pet projects their representatives want for their district."

"Okay, do that. But let's not act on that until we have to," the president said. Just then, the buzzer went off. Harrison pressed his intercom button. He said, "Yes? What is it?"

His secretary responded, "Mr. Banner from the FBI is here. He said you wanted to see him for an update on Mr. Bigelow's murder."

"Yes! Send him in."

Harrison turned to Paul Barrows. "I hope he's got something."

Clive Banner came in. "Good morning, Mr. President. Hello, Paul," he said.

"Good morning, Clive," responded Harrison. Paul just nodded. "Sit on the couch. Tell me, have you got any leads?"

Clive said, "I'm afraid not, sir."

"Well, what have you got?"

"Mr. President, I have over two-dozen agents working on this case. We went back to the house. The forensic team went through the whole house in case the murderer went to other rooms. They went outside to look for footprints and to double-check if the perpetrator gained entry through a window. We found nothing except some powder on the doorknobs and smeared fingerprints of the family members. Apparently, the murderer used latex gloves to avoid leaving fingerprints. The forensic team says the powder is the kind you find on painters' latex gloves. The report from the medical examiner says the gun was right up against the victims' heads. He says the powder on the heads of the victims is consistent with the gun being held right at the victims' heads. The fact that the shots were not heard by the daughter indicates the perp used a silencer."

"So you found nothing new?" the president asked.

"That's right. I believe this was a professional killer. He is one smart cookie."

"Have you found a motive?"

"No. We talked to all your White House personnel. Everyone says Bigelow got along with everyone. No one can recall any disagreement with him. We talked to all his friends. We went through his phone book and talked to all of them. Everyone liked the man. To the best of our ability, we could not find an enemy or someone with a grudge. He was well liked."

"How about his computer? He sent and received a lot of emails."

"The lab went through his files and hard drive and found nothing out of the normal mail traffic—except one-mail he sent the day he was murdered."

"What was that about?"

"He sent an e-mail to your director of national security, Benjamin Goodman, and the senate majority leader, George Paxton."

"What's so unusual about that? The White House converses a lot with those two men," Harrison responded, a little taken aback.

"It isn't whom he sent the e-mail to, but the content of it. Have you ever heard of a bill or program called Eagle Down?"

Harrison thought for a moment then shook his head and said, "I can't say that I have. Have you, Paul?"

Paul said, "No. I've never heard of it. If it were a bill, I surely would have heard of it. Or any program the House or Senate would have proposed, for that matter."

"What did the e-mail say?" the president asked.

Clive said, "It said one of Saxton's assistants mentioned something about Eagle Down. Then the assistant said it concerned national security and he couldn't talk about it. And Bigelow asked what the program was about."

"Did Either Saxton or Goodman respond?"

"No. I suppose Bigelow was murdered before they could. I went over to the Senate and talked to Saxton, but he said he was puzzled and had no idea what Bigelow was talking about. I got the same response from Goodman."

"Do you think it could have something do with his murder?" Harrison asked.

"Can't tell until I know what this Eagle Down is. One of the best leads an investigator has is motive. If you have motive, it will generally lead you to the killer. In this case, we have no motive. So we don't know where to look."

"Okay, Clive, keep digging and let me know if you get a lead."

With that comment, Clive left. Harrison sat down on the couch and murmured, "Eagle Down. What could that be?" Then he turned to Paul. "That's puzzling, Paul. Ask around and see if anyone in the White House has heard of it."

* * *

That morning, Carol and Bob went in to see Sam Corcoran. He was reading an article that one of his reporters had written. He liked to smoke cigars and had a newly lit cigar in his mouth. He looked up when Carol and Bob came in his office. He took the cigar out of his mouth and looked over the top of his glasses. He said, "Well, what did you get? Did you sleep with him?"

"No! I didn't sleep with him. We had a nice dinner at Oscar's."

"But did you learn anything?"

"He told me things we already knew and said the forensic team didn't turn up anything and they have no leads."

"That's it? Nothing else?" Sam said, obviously exasperated.

"Yes. One thing."

"Well, spit it out. Is it important?"

"He said the forensic lab found an e-mail that was sent to the senate majority leader and the director of national security asking about a bill or a program called Eagle Down. And no one seems to know anything about a bill or program called that."

"Hmm. Eagle Down. Sounds like something to do with bird preservation."

Carol responded, "The FBI director, Clive Banner, talked to both men, and they pleaded ignorance of the bill or program."

"When was the e-mail sent?"

"The day Bigelow was murdered."

"Now, isn't that a coincidence? Okay, you guys, run it down. Talk to everyone in the House and Senate if you have to. But find out what that bill or program is. I have a hunch that it has something to do with Bigelow's murder. Now get out of here and go to work," Sam ordered.

He put the cigar back in his mouth and continued reading the article.

Carol and Bob went back to their desks and sat down. Bob sat looking at the ceiling then abruptly bolted to his desk. He exclaimed, "I've got it, Carol! If we follow the chief's idea, we will be weeks—maybe months—talking to the whole Congress."

"Maybe more. That's almost five hundred and fifty people."

"So why don't we put it in the next article we write on the murder? How shall we phrase it? Let's say the FBI has found an e-mail on the murdered man's computer referring to a bill or program called Eagle Down and has no idea what the bill or program is. And if anyone has heard of it or knows what the program is, call the FBI or the paper. How's that?"

Carol thought for a moment, then she said, "Should work. I'm sure all the House and Senate members read our paper every day. Okay, let's go with it."

They sat down at the computer and began to write the story. It would be on page 1, with the story headed up by the line in bold print: fbi stymied. Of course, with both their names. The story carried the entire investigation of the FBI and what they had discovered. Instead of using Dan Morris's name as the source of the information, they cited sources from within the FBI. Then the story said an e-mail from Bigelow's computer referred to the phrase "Eagle Down" and the FBI was at a loss to understand the meaning of that phrase. If anyone had any information or knowledge of that phrase, they were asked to contact the FBI or the newspaper.

Carol and Bob took the article to Sam. He read it and said, "Okay, let the story go as you've written it. *But* if it gets no results, then I want you to get on your hiking boots and go over to Congress. Got it?"

"Got it, Chief," they said in unison.

CHAPTER 2

The *Washington Ledger* newspaper hit the street, and Bob and Carol waited to see if they got any calls. The next morning, Carol phoned Dan Morris at his office. When Dan answered, she said, "Bob and I put that phrase 'Eagle Down' in our article in yesterday's paper to see if we got any response from anyone. We didn't. Did you get any response on it?"

"No, but you got me in a lot of trouble, Carol. The director knew you and I had been lovers a while back, and when he saw that Eagle Down story in the paper under your byline, he knew I told you about that e-mail. He really burned my tail for giving you that information."

"I'm sorry, Dan, but that's the only lead you and the police have. I wanted to get it out in the public and see if anyone knew something about it."

"Well, so far, we got zilch. Nothing. So all your story got was a peck of trouble for me. If you get any feedback on the story, you be sure to call me first. Maybe if we get some response from the article, I can smooth over the director's feathers."

"Will do, Dan. And again, I'm sorry I got you in hot water. You know I would never divulge my source of information to anyone."

"I know, but the director figured that one out all by himself. He didn't need to ask you if I gave that information to you," Dan said.

When Carol hung up, Bob asked, "Did he get any calls?"

"No. But he said the director knew he gave me that Eagle Down tip and got his tail burned for it. So what if we don't get any calls? Where do we go next? Congress?"

"I guess."

"Bob, if that article doesn't bring any results, what good will it do to question the House of Representatives and the Senate? They all read the paper."

"Probably none. But if Sam says do it, we do it."

They waited two more days, and no calls were made to the FBI or the paper. They were getting anxious. They were not looking forward to questioning all the members of Congress.

Then, on the morning of the fourth day, Carol's phone rang. She quickly picked it up, hoping it was a call about Eagle Down. When she answered, a woman's voice said, "Hello. Is this Carol Williams?"

"Yes, it is. How can I help you?"

"You had a story in your paper a few days ago about something called Eagle Down."

"Yes, I did. Do you have any information about that?"

"Yes!" the woman responded excitedly.

Carol started banging her pen on her desk to get Bob's attention. When he looked over, she pointed to his telephone. He picked it up to hear a woman's voice say, "I know what that project is."

Carol looked at Bob and smiled broadly, and he smiled back. She said, "Okay, what is Eagle Down?"

"Oh, I can't tell you over the phone. This is too hush-hush. I work in the majority leader's office in the Senate, and I have a folder with the complete program called Eagle Down. I copied it, but I wasn't supposed to see it. I can give it to you, but you cannot tell anyone where you got it. Can you do that?"

"You betcha. We never reveal our sources. Can I pick up the folder?"

"No. I would rather we meet somewhere, and I can give it to you. I don't want anyone to see me with you. I have the folder in my safe-deposit box. I'll have to go to the bank first," the lady said.

"Fine, just name the time and place. By the way, what is your name?"

"Patricia Manning. Why don't we meet in a cafeteria on Twenty-Third Street near H Avenue for lunch tomorrow at noon? No, make that twelve fifteen. It's a restaurant called Quick Stop. Would that be convenient?"

"Yes, Patricia. Noon tomorrow. How shall I recognize you?"

Patricia said, "I'll be wearing a tan suit. Besides, I've seen your picture in your paper many times. I will recognize you."

"Fine. I'll see you tomorrow, Patricia."

"Remember, you don't know where you got the folder. My life could be in danger if you told anyone where you got it."

As Carol talked to the woman, she made notes of the conversation. Then she hung up the phone, looked at Bob, clapped her hands, and said, "Bingo!"

Bob smiled and said, "We did it. Now we can scoop all the papers and TV networks. Do you know where that cafeteria is?"

"I haven't been there, but I know the location. Maybe we both should go."

"I have no problem with that. Maybe Patricia will tell us how she came to get ahold of this hush-hush document. Didn't she say she worked in the majority leader's office?" Bob said.

"Yes."

"But Dan told you that the majority leader never heard of the Eagle Down project."

Carol said, "That's right. So did the director of national security. Something is funny here. Why would two top men in the government deny knowing anything about a project that even the president doesn't know about? Something is strange here."

"Let's wait until we get a look at the project. That might help us understand."

They went into Sam's office. Sam looked up but didn't say a word.

Carol said, "Chief, we hit pay dirt."

"You did? And what might that be?"

"I got a call from a woman named"—she looked down at her pad to see the woman's name, which she had written down—"Patricia Manning. She said she works in the senate majority leader's office and has a folder about a project called Eagle Down. She said she would give it to me tomorrow. I'm to meet her just after noon at a cafeteria in town."

"Terrific! Good work. Hmm. I thought the senate majority leader knew nothing about that project? Did she say she got it from his office?"

"No," said Carol, looking at her notes. "She just said she worked there. She didn't say where she got the folder, but she copied it and it was very hush-hush. She must have gotten it out of the majority leader's office. How else could she get ahold of it? One other thing she said was her life could be in danger. Sounds ominous."

"Well, when you meet her tomorrow, quiz her and find out where she got it and how she came to see it if it's so hush-hush. Don't print any of this until we get our hands on the folder," Sam demanded.

"What about Dan Morris of the FBI, my friend? Can I notify him that I have a lead?"

"No, damn it. Wait until we get the folder and see what's in it. Then we can decide whom to tell, if anyone. This could be a national secret, some mysterious military project. If it's evidence relating to the Bigelow murders, then we are obligated by law to turn it over to the authorities. Since we don't have anything new on the Bigelow murders, I'm putting a follow-up story on page 2 for this afternoon's edition. So write it up that way. See what the daughter has to say. We haven't covered that angle yet. And keep that Eagle Down angle in the story. We could get another hit. And good work. Now go."

They went back to the Bigelow residence and knocked on the door. A woman in her fifties answered. "Yes?"

"Good afternoon, madam. I'm Carol Williams, and this is Bob Grant. We are from the *Washington Ledger*. We would like to talk to Caroline. Can we see her?"

"That girl is still in shock. She's talked to the police and the FBI and is in distress over her parents being murdered. I'm her aunt. Can't you leave her alone?"

"I promise we won't upset her. We have just a few questions for her. Then we will leave. It will just take a minute," Carol responded as politely as she could.

"Okay, but just a minute. She's up in her room. I'll get her. Wait in the living room."

The woman went upstairs and, a minute later, came down with Caroline behind her.

When they came into the living room, Carol smiled and said, "Hello, Caroline. I'm Carol Williams, and this man is Bob Grant. We are from the newspaper the *Washington Ledger*. I know you have been through a very traumatic experience, so I won't take too much of your time."

Caroline never said a word, just listened with a stoic look on her face.

Carol went on. "On the night your parents were killed, did you hear any noise at all, like a firecracker going off or someone walking down the stairs?"

Caroline never said a word, just shook her head no.

"Did you know all of your parents' friends?"

She nodded.

"Were any of them mad at your dad or mom?"

She shrugged, as if to say she didn't know.

"Caroline," Carol went on, "did you see anyone around the house, on the sidewalk, or maybe sitting in a car the day your parents were killed?"

Caroline shook her head no and then started to sob. The aunt said to Carol, "That's enough. You've upset the child. You'd better go."

"Maybe you're right, madam. Thanks, Caroline. And good day to both of you."

They left and went back to the office to write a follow-up story to the double homicide.

* * *

At five o'clock that day, Patricia Manning closed her desk, locked it, picked up her handbag, and left the building to go home. She rode the bus to and from work every day. The bus stop was only a few blocks from the building in which she worked. She lived in an apartment in a town in Virginia called Chantilly, about twenty-five miles from Washington, DC. Usually, she got off the bus and took a local bus to her house, which let her off with only a few blocks to walk to her apartment. This night, however, she needed groceries, so she got off the bus near a supermarket, did her shopping, then took a cab to her apartment. When she got home, she checked her mailbox. There was nothing but advertisements in it.

When she got in her apartment, she turned on the TV to the news channel. She was about to start making her dinner, but the news broadcast was talking about the Bigelow murders, so she fixed herself a glass of wine and sat down to listen to the TV. Then the news went on to talk about the debate raging in the Senate and the House of Representatives about the bill that the president wanted passed for a spending plan of one and a half trillion dollars. She was tired from the day's work, and after she finished her glass of wine, she fell asleep in the chair.

She woke up, and it was past nine o'clock. She felt hungry, so she started her dinner on the stove. As she was cooking, she heard a knock on her door. She wondered who that could be. She went to the door and opened it. Standing there was a tall man dressed in black clothes, with a thin black mustache and a goatee. He was wearing latex gloves. He looked evil, and she became frightened and said in a quivering voice, "Yes, can I help you?"

Without saying a word, the man pushed her back into the apartment, knocking her down. She sat on her butt, astonished and frightened. He closed the door, walked over to the frightened woman, reached behind to his back, and took out a Beretta with a silencer from his waistband. He pushed the gun up to her forehead as she sat on the floor frightened and quivering.

The man said in a growling voice, "Where is the Eagle Down folder?"

She replied with a great amount of fear in her voice and the gun at her forehead. "I don't have it here. It's in my bank."

"Don't lie to me, lady. We know you have it. Now give it to me!"

"I'm telling you, I don't have it here."

"Lady, I'm going to ask you one more time, give me the folder, or you'll get a bullet in your head."

"Oh, please don't shoot me! Please don't shoot me! Please! I'll get the folder for you tomorrow. You can go to the bank with me, but please, please don't shoot me."

The killer was amused at Patricia pleading for her life. He was sent to kill her and find the folder. He thought she was lying. He had no compunctions about killing her and would search her apartment. Without another word, the man pulled the trigger on his gun, shooting Patricia in the forehead. The muffled sound of the silencer was not heard outside the apartment. The bullet entered her brain. She fell back with her eyes wide open, staring at the ceiling. She was dead when she hit the floor. The killer laughed as he looked at the surprised look on Patricia's face. Then he looked around at the apartment and began a thorough search of it.

He pulled out every drawer in the kitchen and spilled all the contents on the floor. He opened every cabinet and pulled the dishes out, and they fell and broke on the kitchen floor. He felt the shelves, hoping to find the folder. He looked in the refrigerator and the oven. Then he went into her bedroom, took all the clothes out of the closet, and threw them on the floor. He opened the dresser drawers and threw the clothes on the floor. He looked in the nightstand and, finally, lifted the mattress, looking for the folder. Then he went into the living room. He cut the sofa and an easy chair with a knife. He looked on top of a china cabinet and in a drawer in it. He bent down and looked under the couch. Finally, he decided the folder was not in the apartment, so he left, closing the door behind him. When he got in his car, he dialed a number on his cell phone. It rang three times, and someone answered.

"Hello?"

He said, "She's dead, but the folder was not in her apartment. She said it was in a safety deposit box in her bank."

"Okay, drop it. If I want you to follow up on getting it, I'll call you."

Then the killer hung up.

The food Patricia put on the stove was beginning to burn. It put out a black smoke, and as the smoke reached the living room, the fire alarm in the living room's ceiling went off. When it didn't stop, the neighbors in the upstairs apartment finally went down and knocked on Patricia's door. When they got no answer and could smell the smoke, they went back upstairs and dialed 911 to report the fire.

In just a few minutes, a fire engine and a paramedic van drove up to the apartment complex. The neighbors who called 911 directed the firemen to Patricia's apartment. When they reached the door, they saw black smoke coming from under the door. They banged loudly on the door. After thirty seconds, when no one opened it, they took their axe, broke the lock on the door, and went in. They immediately saw a fire in the kitchen and promptly put it out with a fire extinguisher. Inspecting the rest of the apartment, they saw a woman's body on the living room floor. They checked to see if she was alive and saw the bullet wound to her head and blood on the floor from her wound.

"She's dead," said one of the firemen, bending over her. "She was shot. We better call homicide."

Fifteen minutes later, two homicide detectives from the city of Chantilly—detectives Gary Wilson and Ed Hamburg—arrived at the apartment. The firemen were still there, cleaning up the kitchen stove, when the two detectives walked in and saw the body of Patricia lying on the living room floor. One detective went over to the body, bent over it, and moved her head back and forth, inspecting the wound with his latex-gloved hand. He said, "Looks like one slug to the head, Ed. Can't see any other marks, clothes are not torn, so it doesn't look like a rape."

Then he stood up and surveyed the apartment. "Damn, look at this place. It looks like a hurricane went through here."

"Yeah," said his partner. "It was either a burglar, or he was looking for something after he shot her."

"Okay, Ed, call the crime scene boys. They ought to find something in this mess."

As they spoke, the medical examiner arrived. He gave the body a quick survey and said, "Looks like one bullet to the head. Can't have been dead too long. The body is still warm."

"Anything else, Doc?"

"No, not until I get her back to the morgue and do an autopsy. If nothing else, the bullet to her head would have killed her instantly."

* * *

The morning papers in Chantilly carried a story of a woman murdered. It didn't give her name. The story was not picked up by the national news media. It was just a local homicide. The police don't release the names of victims to the local news media until the next of kin are notified of the victim's death.

Near noon, Carol picked up her handbag and said to Bob, "Let's go. I don't want to get there late. She might leave."

He followed her out to the car. They parked in a parking lot and had to walk several blocks to the cafeteria. Inside, they sat down at a table with a view of the entrance. Bob went and got two cups of coffee for them. It was just past noon. They sat and drank their coffee, and as he sipped his cup, Bob asked Carol, "How did she say she would be dressed?"

"In a tan suit."

"Any hat or something else?"

"No. She just said a tan suit."

They waited. Bob looked at the clock on the wall. It read twelve thirty, then twelve forty-five.

"I don't think she's going to show, Carol. She said around twelve."

"Give her a chance. She said she had to go to the bank. She could have been held up there or caught in traffic."

Bob went and got another cup of coffee. They sat and waited. Finally, at one thirty, Bob said, "Give it up, Carol. She isn't going to show. Let's go!"

"I think you're right. Okay, maybe it was too good to be true. When we get back to the office, I'm going to try and call her."

When they got back to the office, Carol called the Senate office building in which the majority leader was housed. When the operator answered, she asked for Patricia Manning. The phone rang seven times. Finally, a woman's voice came on the line. "Patricia Manning's desk. Can I help you?"

"Yes," said Carol. "I would like to speak to Ms. Manning."

The woman said in response, "I'm sorry, she isn't in today."

"When will she be in?"

"I don't know. She was supposed to be here today, but she didn't show up for work."

"Is she sick?"

"I don't know. Her supervisor called her home but couldn't get in touch with her. You could try again tomorrow. Can I help you?"

"No. I want to talk with Patricia. Can you give me her home phone?"

"No. I'm sorry. We are not permitted to give out personal information on employees. Try again tomorrow. Give me your name and phone number, and I'll have her call you when she comes in."

Carol gave her name and phone number. When she hung up, she looked at Bob. "She isn't in today, and they don't know why. They won't give me her phone number. They said try tomorrow. So all we can do is wait."

"You know, that woman could have been pulling your leg, maybe wanting to get her name in the paper. It's possible."

"You could be right. But I think she was genuine. I just have a gut feeling that she's on to something."

"Well, let's tell Sam before he calls us in," Bob said.

They walked into Sam's office. He looked up and said, "I don't see you carrying any folder. Did you meet your mystery woman?"

"No," said Carol. "She didn't show up."

"So it was a wild-goose chase?"

"I don't think so. I called her office, and she didn't report for work today. She could have gotten sick or into an accident, or maybe she is in the hospital."

"'Yeah, and maybe strawberries grow on trees. Okay, I'll give you forty-eight hours to find this woman. After that, drop it. I don't want you guys to waste your time beating a dead horse. Now get out of here."

They went back to their desks. Carol sat there in deep thought, and after a few minutes, she looked at her notes on the phone conversation with Patricia then said to Bob, "You know, Patricia said her life could be in danger. I wonder if anything happened to her."

"Wouldn't it be in the papers or on your police monitor or the TV news if she met with foul play?"

"Maybe. We don't know what town she lived in, so we don't know what paper or local TV station to watch. It wouldn't be on the police monitor if it was in another town. Don't most federal employees get a once-over by the FBI?"

Bob said, "Yes. But if the job is just clerical, I doubt it."

"I think I'll call Dan. He might know."

"Suit yourself."

Carol dialed the phone number for the FBI office and asked for Dan Morris. When he came on the line, she asked him, "Do you agents do a background check on all federal employees?"

"Not all, Carol. Why do you ask?"

"I want to get in touch with a woman that works in the senate majority leader's office. She is not at work, and I'm worried about her."

"Don't you have her phone number?"

"No."

"Well, look it up in the phone book."

"I can't. I don't know what town she lives in."

"If you don't know her phone number or where she lives, she can't be a friend. You must want this information for your paper."

"Yes, that's true. But it's important. It has to do with Eagle Down."

"Hold on. I got my tail burned on this once before when I told you about the Bigelow e-mail, and now you want me to help you again?"

"Dan, this is important. I think it's a hot lead to the story about Eagle Down. It could help solve the Bigelow murders."

"Before I help you again, I want to know what you know. Meet me in your cafeteria in half an hour, and let's talk."

"Okay. I'll bring Bob Grant, my partner," Carol said.

"Bring whomever you want. But level with me."

* * *

Bob and Carol were sitting in the cafeteria when Dan walked in. He sat down and said hello to Carol, who introduced him to Bob. "Now, what's this hot lead you talked about?" he asked after pleasantries were exchanged.

"After we put the story out about the Bigelow murders, we inserted the phrase Eagle Down and asked anyone who knew about that phrase to call your office or the paper."

"Yeah, I remember that. My ass is still scorching from the director's blast for giving you that information. So what's the hot lead?"

"Two days ago, a woman phoned me and said she had a folder about Eagle Down. She said she copied it from the majority leader's office and would turn it over to me. She sounded scared and said her life may be in danger. We agreed to meet in town at a cafeteria at noon yesterday and she would give me the folder. But she never showed up."

"It sounds like she was looking for fifteen minutes of fame. She probably wasn't legit."

"No, I think she was. Anyway, I called this morning to her office, and they said she didn't show up for work. They tried to get in touch with her, but she didn't answer her phone. I think something has happened to her."

"Carol, you realize that if it's true and she does have a folder on Eagle Down, you will be obligated to turn it over to the authorities. That's the law."

"I know, but it will give the paper an exclusive and maybe help you solve the Bigelow murders."

"That assumes the folder of Eagle Down is related to the homicides."

"Of course. Will you help us?"

"Tell you what. If you give me the name of this woman, I can look her up in our files. If she isn't there, I can go to the Social Security office computer and get her address from their files. If not there, then the Internal Revenue files. But I will go with you to see this woman. If she has a file like you describe, I will let you read it, but I take it back as evidence. Deal?"

"Deal," replied Carol. They shook hands in agreement, and Dan left.

* * *

The next morning, Dan called Carol. "Okay, I got the woman's address. She lives in Chantilly in Virginia. I'll stop by your office and pick you and Bob up. Then we can drive there."

Twenty minutes later, Dan drove up to the front entrance of the newspaper's office. Carol and Bob were already waiting outside. They got in, with Carol in the front seat. "Did you have any trouble getting the address, Dan?"

"No. I got if from Social Security. The FBI has access to just about all government records. The town Chantilly is only about twenty minutes from here. Here's the address." He handed Carol a piece of paper. "Also, I copied a map of the town from my computer and marked her address in red on the map. Take the map and be the copilot and direct me when we get to the town."

"I hope the woman is just sick. She could have been in an accident and be in the hospital. That may account for her not answering her phone," said Carol.

"Could be. We'll find out in a few minutes. Look up ahead. There's the turnoff for Chantilly."

They took the turnoff for Chantilly. Carol started giving Dan instructions to drive to Patricia's apartment. Soon, they pulled up in front of a two-story apartment building. She said, "This is it. You have written apartment 5 on your sheet."

They got out, went under a stairway that led up to the second floor, and walked down a walkway to apartment 5. Dan stopped short and said, "Uh-oh." There was yellow plastic tape on the door marked police—do not enter. He saw the lock was broken. "I think we'd better find out what happened here. Maybe one of the neighbors can tell us."

They knocked on several doors, but no one was home. So they went up to the next floor and knocked on the door of the apartment above Patricia's. An elderly woman opened the door. "Yes?" she said.

Dan showed her his FBI credentials. "Madam, I'm Agent Morris of the FBI. I came to see Patricia Manning, but I see there is police tape on her door. Can you tell me what happened?"

"Oh my, yes. She was murdered. It was awful, and her apartment had a fire in it. The firemen and police came. They took her away in a van. I think it said something about a medical something or another."

"Medical examiner?" Dan said.

"Yes, that was it."

"When did this happen?"

"Two nights ago."

"Thank you, madam. You have been a big help."

After that, they went downstairs. Carol asked, "What do we do now, Dan?"

"Call Chantilly homicide, find out what happened, and get them to let us in the apartment to see if there is that folder in there."

Dan dialed information, got the number of the Chantilly police department, and called them. When they answered, he asked for homicide. A man came on and said, "Homicide. Detective Wilson. How can I help you?"

"Detective, this is Agent Morris of the FBI. I understand there was a homicide here in Chantilly two nights ago."

"Yes, there was. What interest does the FBI have in a local murder?"

"I think it might be connected to two other murders in Washington. I came down to see Patricia Manning concerning the murders, and a neighbor told me she was murdered."

"That's right, Morris. Two nights ago. So how can I help you?"

"I would like the details of any evidence you have, and I would like to get into her apartment. I'm looking for something special."

"Where are you?"

"I'm at her apartment complex."

"Okay, stay there. I'll be down in fifteen minutes."

The three waited by the apartment door, chatting. Soon, a police cruiser pulled up to the curb, and two men got out of the car and walked to the apartment door. They walked up, and one of them stuck out his hand. "Agent Morris?"

"Yes," said Dan. "Detective Wilson?" They shook hands, and Wilson introduced his partner. Then Morris introduced Carol and Bob. Detective Wilson tore the yellow police tape off the door and opened it. They all went in.

Dan was surprised at the mess in the apartment. "Damn! What went on here? A big struggle?" he said.

"No. We think the murderer was looking for something and tore up the place trying to find it." Wilson then walked over to chalk lines on the rug and, pointing at them, said, "This is where she was shot."

"What have you got so far, Wilson?"

"Not much. The way we figure it is the woman was cooking dinner and someone came to the door. She let him in."

"How do you know that, Detective?" asked Carol.

"The door and windows weren't jimmied, and the only other way is to use a key. Anyway, she lets the assailant in. He wants something. What, we don't know. She doesn't give it to him. So he shoots her then tears up the apartment looking for whatever."

"What about the fire?" asked Dan.

"We figure she was cooking, and when she got shot, the gas was under the food and burned."

"What about the weapon?"

"ME says it was a nine-millimeter slug. She died instantly. He held the gun against her head, considering the powder burns on her forehead. He must have used a silencer. No one heard a gunshot. The upstairs neighbors heard the fire alarm going off. They came down but couldn't get an answer, so they called 911. End of story."

"A nine-millimeter slug? That's the same as our case in Georgetown."

"Georgetown? Are you talking about the Bigelow homicide?"

"Yes. Detective, I would like to take that slug back with me and turn it over to our ballistics lab and have them match it against the slugs taken from the Bigelows. I'm convinced these two cases are connected in some way."

"You got it, Morris. Follow me back to the station."

"Okay," Dan said.

"Just a minute, Dan. Aren't you going to search the apartment for the folder?" asked Carol.

"What folder?" asked Detective Wilson.

Dan answered, "We came down not only to talk to Patricia but to pick up a folder she had about a new project the government was working on."

"Well, be my guest. But you can see someone beat you to it. Do you think the killer was after the same folder?"

"Could be."

"That could be the motive for the killing," said Wilson. "Again, Detective, could be."

They drove back to Washington, DC. Dan dropped Carol and Bob off, and he went to the forensic lab and gave them the slug taken from Patricia's head. He told them to compare that slug with the ones removed from the Bigelows' bodies and see if it matched. Later in the day, he got a call from the forensic lab. The slug from Patricia's body matched the slugs taken from the Bigelows'.

The next morning, he phoned Carol. "Hello, doll. I have news."

"What's that?"

"I'm going to ask you and Bob to come over to my office. I want to see the director, and I want you to accompany me."

"The director of the FBI?"

"Yep. Clive Banner himself."

"Sure! You bet! Is there a story in this?"

"I'll leave it up to Banner. If he okays it, you can print the story. But if he says keep it under wraps, then you must agree to do so. Fair enough?"

"Fair enough!" Carol said, excited.

She hung up and threw a pencil at Bob, hitting a paper he was reading. "Let's go. Dan is inviting us to talk to Clive Banner about the Bigelow murders."

"The director of the FBI?"

"Yep, none other."

When they got to the FBI building, they went in and were directed to Dan's desk. Dan greeted them. "Glad you could make it. Let's go upstairs."

Outside the director's door, his secretary told them to go in and that Banner was expecting them. When they came into the office, Banner stood up and came around his desk.

"Mr. Banner," Dan said, "these are the two reporters from the *Washington Ledger* I told you about. They led me to some startling information. So I thought it appropriate that they hear what I have to tell you. This is Carol Williams, and this gentleman is Bob Grant."

"Glad to meet you. Sit down. Now, what do you have that is so important?"

"If you recall, we have no motive for the murders of Bigelow and his wife." Banner nodded, and Dan went on. "All our lab found at the crime scene was powder from latex gloves on the doorknobs. The slugs taken from the victims were nine millimeters."

"That's correct," Banner replied.

"The police—and us, for that matter—could find no motive for the murders. We interviewed hundreds of people, friends and business associates, and got the same answer: Bigelow was well liked and had no enemies. The only item that could not be explained was an e-mail sent by Bigelow on the day he was murdered. He sent the e-mail to the senate majority leader and the director of national security."

"Yes, I recall. I personally talked to both of them. They said they had no knowledge of any bill or project called Eagle Down."

"Well, sir, I'm not so sure of that."

"What do you mean?" the FBI director asked, surprised.

"I think the majority leader does know about that project."

"Are you saying one of the highest members of our government lied to the FBI? That's a felony. Can you prove it?"

"No. But hear me out. I inadvertently slipped and told Ms. Williams here about the e-mail—"

"Yes, and that was a breach of trust on your part."

"Yes, sir. And I apologize for that. Anyway, she put that information in the paper in an article about the Bigelow homicides and asked anyone with knowledge of the Eagle Down project to call the FBI or the paper. In a few days, a woman called Ms. Williams. She said she knew of the project and had a folder with papers about the Eagle Down project she copied from the majority leader's office. She agreed to turn them over to her the next day at a cafeteria in the city. She never showed up. She was murdered that night in her apartment with a gun that shoots nine-millimeter bullets, with a silencer—the same weapon used in the Bigelow murders. The assailant tore up her apartment, presumably looking for the folder."

"Did he find it?"

"We don't know. But I took the slug used in killing her and gave it to our ballistics lab for comparison to the slugs taken from the Bigelows', and they matched."

"Really?"

"So two things tie the two murders together: the gun and the Eagle Down project."

"Dan, that makes sense. So we have a professional killer on the loose, killing anyone who has anything to do with that project," Clive responded.

"Yes, sir. That's the way it appears to me."

"Other than the murdered woman who worked in the majority leader's office, do you have anything at all that shows he knows about the project?"

"No, sir. But I feel he's involved in some way."

"Now, hold on. We can't accuse one of our government's highest officials of complicity in murder without any proof." Then, turning to Carol and Bob, he said, "That also goes for you and your paper."

"Can we print that the two murders are tied together by the Eagle Down folder?" Carol asked.

"Yes. That might bring some termites out of the woodwork. But both of you watch your back. If this is true, whoever is behind this will come after you, and we can't give you twenty-four-hour protection."

"We will. And thank you, Mr. Banner," Carol said. Then they left Banner's office.

* * *

Carol and Bob went right to Sam's office. He was sitting in his office, watching television. When they walked in, he said, "Sit down and watch this. Some private pilot crashed into a house in Virginia. It was a twin-engine plane. Killed him and an occupant in her house. Damn fools. Okay, what have you two got?"

Carol smiled. "You won't believe this!"

"No? Try me."

"Remember the woman that was going to give me a folder about Eagle Down?"

"Yeah."

"Well, we found her."

"Terrific. Did you get the folder?"

"No."

"No? Goddamnit! Did she have it?"

"We don't know."

"What kind of game is this? She has it, she doesn't have it. Does it exist at all?"

"We really don't know."

"What kind of reporters are you two? You let a woman take you on a merry-go-round. I have it. No, I don't have it. Guess if it exists. Rubbish."

"Hang on, Chief. The woman that said she had the folder was murdered the night before she was to give me the folder."

"What? Murdered! Where? How?" Sam said, clearly surprised.

"She lived in Chantilly, Virginia, about twenty or thirty miles from here, in her apartment. She was shot, and her apartment was torn up. It looks like the killer was looking for the folder. We don't know if he found it. And get this: the same gun that killed the Bigelows killed the woman. How's that for coincidence?"

"Damn! Now that's a story. Okay, get on it! I want it front page and the banner reading, murders tied together."

***

Not long after the afternoon papers hit the street—he was sitting in his room in a hotel, reading the paper about the murders—the killer's phone rang. He picked it up and said, "Yes?"

A man's voice said, "You read the paper?"

"Yes."

"Those reporters are getting too close. Follow them, see where they go, and call me every night. If they get too close, you will have to take them out."

"Got it."

"And get another gun. Your bullets can be identified. Throw the old one in the Potomac."

"Will do," the killer said, and the caller hung up.

***

The House of Representatives and the Senate were debating the one-and-a-half-trillion-dollar stimulus bill that President Gerald Harrison wanted passed. The debate in both houses looked like a stalemate, and the bill would not pass. So he arranged for the majority senate leader, George Saxton, and the house speaker, Samuel Giddings, to come to his office for a meeting to see if he could break the ice and get the bill brought to a vote. Also in the meeting was Paul Barrows, the president's chief of staff. They met in the oval office.

"Gentlemen," Harrison said, starting the meeting, "you know why I called this meeting. The stimulus bill is stalled in both the House and the Senate. I want to figure out a way to get the bill to a vote. We need this bill to get the country out of this recession. If we don't, we will fall into a deeper recession and maybe a depression like the 1930s, and that will destroy this country. The unemployment rate is at an all-time high, except for the 1930s. People are losing their houses, and Social Security is now spending forty billion more than it takes in. We have to act and act quickly. Any ideas?"

"Mr. President," Saxton replied, "the problem is that our constituents are riled that we could run this country into a deficit so large it will cause a financial calamity. They say we are putting this financial burden on our children and grandchildren. The members of the Senate and the House are afraid that if they vote for the bill, they will be voted out of office in the midterm elections."

"George, I was voted into office with 52.5 percent of the popular vote. I campaigned with the stimulus bill as my main platform. If the people were against the bill, I wouldn't have been elected to office. I don't think that's the problem."

"Mr. President," Giddings said, "the polls show that 55 percent of the people polled were against this bill."

"Sam, you and I know polls change from day to day."

"Mr. President, if we shelve this bill for the time being and get a bill to reduce taxes, your bill may stand a better chance later," said Paxton.

"You really believe that? If we reduce taxes, as your party proposed in the campaign, reduce our income tax proceeds, and then pass a stimulus bill, we will have a much bigger deficit than just my bill alone. No, that's not the answer, George. Let's keep our eye on the ball here. I want that bill passed, and I want you men to find a way to get it passed. Take a poll and find out where you stand. Surely, some of the holdouts have something they want. Promise them earmarks for their district or state. But stop the debate and get an up or down vote. Keeping the debate going and giving the news media a field day is not helping. I'm convinced this bill will create jobs in the government sector and small business sector. It will give loans to small businesses and give banks money to lend to get the economy going again. Hell, small businesses create more jobs than government and big businesses combined."

The meeting went on for another hour before the two leaders left. Harrison just sat there without saying anything after they left. Paul sat there looking at the president. Then he finally spoke. "You know, Mr. President, both those men are against your bill. Their party is strongly against it. I don't think they are working for its passage. It's going to take a miracle to get your bill passed."

Harrison looked at Paul with his eyes narrowed. "I know, but we have to keep after them. I think there are enough votes in our party to pass the bill, but it has to be brought to a vote. Get the House and Senate minority leaders up here. Let me have a talk with them."

CHAPTER 3

George Saxton and Samuel Giddings sat in Saxton's office discussing the meeting with the president. "What are we going to do, George? The president will know if we hold back on the vote."

"Not in the Senate. I'll have one of our party's senators start a filibuster. Hell, we can keep it going for a long time. All the president's party senators are not yet in his camp. I have a few that have doubts. I'll work on them."

"Won't that get back to the White House?"

"No. I'll keep it low-key."

"And if we can't stop a vote?"

"Then we activate Eagle Down."

"I thought that was a last resort?"

"Let me assure you, Sam, it will be. In the end, if the stimulus bill passes, it will be the end of the United States being a dominant world power. The deficit will grow so large no country will buy our bonds for fear we will default. China buys a huge quantity now, but if they see our deficit get to be a bigger percent of our GDP, they'll know we cannot sustain our economy. Then where will we get money? Print more? That will cause our economy to go into an upward, increased inflation spiral, causing consumers to spend less. It will put our economy into a downward spiral, causing increased unemployment." He paused for a moment then added, "We have to defeat this bill, Sam, and propose a reduction in taxes. We have to put money in the hands of the consumers. Their spending is 70 percent of our GDP. If they spend, factories will start hiring again to produce the goods consumers want and build up their inventories. It seems so elementary. I can't see why this administration can't see it."

"The economists advising the administration don't see it that way, George," replied Samuel.

"Sam, we've got some of the best academic economists in the land. They say the president's plan will cause an economic disaster. We have to stop this bill, come hell or high water."

* * *

The next morning, Ted Sampson, the minority house leader, and John Pearson, the senate minority leader, were in the oval office. Sitting with them was Paul Barrows, chief of staff. They were waiting for the president. Shortly, Harrison walked in. "Sorry to keep you waiting, gentlemen, but General Winters was giving me an update on our military operations."

He sat down opposite the three men. "I don't suppose I have to tell you why I asked you to come here. I had the house speaker and the majority leader here yesterday. We had a long discussion on how to pass the stimulus bill. I know they are against it as well as their party, but we have to get this bill passed. What is the tally of votes? Do you think there are enough to pass?"

Ted, the house leader, spoke first. "Mr. President, I believe everyone in our party will vote for the bill. But that won't be enough to pass it. We are going to need at least thirty votes from the other party."

"Can we get them?"

"At first, I thought there were more than that. But the speaker has been twisting arms, trying to get those who might vote for the bill to change their mind."

"How about you, John?"

"Same here. When the bill was first introduced, I thought we had enough votes to pass, but George Saxton has been getting to his party members. I think he has changed some minds. I don't have an exact count, but it's close."

"Okay, talk to the members you think are on the fence. See what it would take to get them to support the bill and get back to me," Harrison ordered.

"You mean offer them earmarks?"

The president responded, "Of course. This will help them in the midterm elections. They always brag about bringing government dollars to their district when they are campaigning."

* * *

Carol and Bob were sitting in Sam's office, discussing the Bigelow murders.

"Let's go over what we know," said Sam. "The gun that shot the Bigelows was the same gun that shot Patricia Manning. And the e-mail that Bigelow sent George Saxton and Benjamin Goodman mentioned the phrase Eagle Down. Patricia said she had a folder that she copied from Saxton's office talking about Eagle Down. In that e-mail, Bigelow said one of Saxton's aides told him about Eagle Down, but it was a national security secret. We have to assume that Saxton knows about Eagle Down since his aide told Bigelow about it and Patricia copied it and she worked in Saxton's office. So we know that the two murders are connected. What we don't know is why."

"Yeah, Sam," said Bob. "But Saxton told the FBI he knew nothing about Eagle Down."

"Then he must be lying," replied Sam.

"Why would the majority leader in the Senate, one of the highest positions in our government, lie to the FBI? That's a felony. Why would he put his career at risk?"

Sam said, "I don't know. But question him."

"I doubt that he will tell us anything after telling the FBI he didn't know anything about Eagle Down, but we have one more avenue we can travel," said Bob.

"What's that?" asked Sam.

"Bigelow's e-mail said one of Saxton's aides told him about Eagle Down. If we knew who he was, we might get him to talk."

"Or her," said Carol.

"Okay, you two get over to the Senate office building and talk to all of Saxton's aides and see if one of them is the aide that talked to Bigelow. But don't let Saxton know you are questioning them. One more thing: talk to Vice Admiral Goodman. He got a copy of the e-mail, and he denied knowing anything about Eagle Down when the FBI questioned him."

"And if that doesn't produce any results, what then?"

"Talk to some of his aides. They might slip and talk. After all, the aide that gave Bigelow the tip said Eagle Down was connected to national security."

* * *

Carol and Bob drove over to the Senate office building. They went to Saxton's office, but he was in a session of the Senate, so they waited for several hours until the Senate retired for the day. When Saxton came back, they stopped him just outside his office.

"Senator, we are from the *Washington Ledger*. Can we have a word with you?"

"Sure," he said, smiling. "What can I do for you?"

"An e-mail sent to you by Harry Bigelow said something about a phrase called Eagle Down. Mr. Bigelow alluded to the fact in that e-mail that the information came from your office," said Carol.

"Miss, I already told the FBI in their investigation of the Bigelow murders that I never saw or heard of that phrase."

"Yes, so I understand. But a woman from your office was murdered, and she said she had a folder with all the details about Eagle Down and the information came from your office."

"I'm sorry, but I don't know of the woman you are talking about. I have quite a number of employees. I doubt that she got that information from my office since I've never heard of that Eagle Down phrase."

"Would one of your aides know about it?"

"Certainly not! Any information in my office, I would know about. Now if you'll excuse me, I have to get to my office."

Carol and Bob started going to the office of each of Saxton's aides. All denied any knowledge of Eagle Down, except one, Jerry Baldwin. When Carol and Bob came into his office, he invited them to sit down. "I'm sorry, I didn't catch your names. And what can I help you with?"

"I'm Carol Williams, and this is Bob Grant. We are from the *Washington Ledger* and would like to ask you a few questions."

"Sure, I'll help you if I can."

"Are you acquainted with the name Patricia Manning?"

"Yes. Poor woman. She worked in our office. I understand she was murdered."

"That's correct. Did you know her well?"

"No, not well. We would see each other and say hello in the hallway, and she would run errands for us aides. But that's about the extent of it."

"Do you know why she was murdered?"

"No. I can't imagine why anyone would want to kill her. She was such a nice lady."

"She had in her possession a folder that contained information about a bill or project called Eagle Down. Have you heard of that phrase before?"

Jerry's face turned ashen. He gulped and started to stutter. "N-n-no. I . . . I have nev-never heard of th-that phrase."

"That's strange, Mr. Baldwin, because Patricia said she copied that information from this office, the senator's office. And an e-mail sent by Harry Bigelow from the president's office to the senator said that one of Senator Saxton's aides told him about a project or bill called Eagle Down. Was it you?" asked Carol.

Suddenly, Jerry stood up. "I'm sorry, but I'm busy. I can't help you. Talk to someone else."

"Mr. Baldwin," Bob said, "I think you know something. Are you afraid to talk about it?"

"I told you I know nothing about that. Now please leave."

Outside Jerry's office, Carol said to Bob, "He's lying. Did you see his face change when I mentioned Eagle Down?"

"Yep. And as soon as you said that, the questioning was over. He knows something, and he is scared to death to say anything."

They went on to question the rest of the aides but got no further information. No one but Jerry Baldwin had ever heard of Eagle Down.

They made an appointment to see Vice Admiral Goodman. When they went into his office, he offered them coffee, which they accepted. "Now, what can I do for the press today? I always like to keep on the good side of the media. God knows we need their support so we can get the appropriations we need and get the support of the public."

"Admiral," said Carol, "we are not here about appropriations or public opinion."

"No? Then what are you here for?"

"You received an e-mail from Harry Bigelow the day he was murdered, in which he wanted to know more about Eagle Down."

"Yes, I did."

"Did you respond to that e-mail?"

"No, of course not. He was murdered before I could."

"What would you have told him?"

"That I've never heard of Eagle Down."

"The aide who told him about Eagle Down said it was a national security issue and couldn't talk about it. Anything that deals with national security has to cross your desk. Isn't that so?"

"Generally speaking, yes."

"Then if Eagle Down concerns national security, why haven't you heard of it?"

"I can't answer that, except to say maybe there is no project called Eagle Down."

"It seems strange that three people—all tied to Eagle Down—have been murdered and no one knows anything about it. Doesn't that seem odd to you, sir?"

"Yes, I suppose so. But that doesn't mean I knew anything about that project. That is, if it exists."

"Oh, I'm sure it exists. But getting someone to talk about it is something else. Thank you for your time, Admiral."

Then they left.

***

Back at the paper's headquarters, Carol told Sam what they found out. "Chief, everyone we talked to denied ever having heard of Eagle Down, except one, an aide in Saxton's office, a young man named Jerry Baldwin. When we went in, he was as amiable as could be, until I mentioned Eagle Down. When I did, his face changed color, and he started stuttering. He changed his tone, said he was busy, and asked us to leave. He's lying. He knows something. But from his reaction, I'd say he was afraid to talk about Eagle Down."

"Did you get anything from Admiral Goodman?" asked Sam.

"No. He denied ever hearing of Eagle Down. I couldn't read his face to see if he was lying. But he flat-out denied ever hearing about Eagle Down."

"Okay, follow up with this Baldwin. Talk to him again, maybe out of the office, in his home. He might feel safe to talk there."

***

When Carol and Bob left the office, they never noticed a black Mercedes following them wherever they went—even to their homes at night. The Mercedes parked down the street from Carol's apartment until she turned out her lights at night and went to sleep. Then the Mercedes left.

The next morning, when Bob came to work, Carol said to him even before he had sat down, "Bob, something came to me last night that might help in discovering who told Harry Bigelow about Eagle Down."

"Oh? What's that?"

"Doesn't the White House keep track of every visitor to see White House personnel?"

"Yes. That's a public record."

"Then if we take a look at that record, we can see who visited Harry Bigelow the day before or the day he sent that email to Saxton and Goodman."

"You're right! Okay, let's go take a look."

They went to the White House and asked to see the visitors record. Looking down the ledger, they found an entry at nine o'clock in the morning, on the day Bigelow was murdered. The name was Jerry Baldwin. "Eureka, Bob! Here it is. It was Jerry Baldwin. He must have told Bigelow on that visit, because Bigelow sent his e-mail that afternoon."

"Now that we have circumstantial evidence that Baldwin told Bigelow about Eagle Down, let's visit him tonight when he's home."

* * *

The Mercedes followed the two reporters to the White House and followed them in as a public visitor. The killer observed them looking at the visitors record. When Carol and Bob left, they failed to put the record back to the current day. They left it open to the day Bigelow was killed. The killer made the observation then followed Bob and Carol back to the newspaper's office.

While he sat in the parking lot, he made a phone call. When the party answered, he said, "The two reporters went to the White House and looked at the visitors record of parties visiting White House personnel."

"What were they after?"

"They looked at the page from the day I took out the Bigelows."

"Anybody on that list that we know?"

"Yeah. One of your aides, Jerry Baldwin."

"Okay, see if they pay him a visit. Then call me."

* * *

That evening at seven o'clock, Carol and Bob rang the bell to Jerry Baldwin's house. His wife answered the door. "Yes?" she said.

"Is Mr. Baldwin in?" Carol asked. "Yes. Can I tell him who's here to see him?"

"Yes, two reporters from the *Washington Ledger*. We talked to him yesterday."

"Just a moment. I'll get him."

When Baldwin came to the door, he said, "You two. I told you yesterday I know nothing about that Eagle Down you asked about."

"Mr. Baldwin, we checked the public record of visitors to White House personnel on the day Mr. Bigelow was murdered. And you, sir, are the only one that visited Mr. Bigelow from Senator Saxton's office. Right after your visit, he sent an e-mail to Senator Saxton and Admiral Goodman. So we think you told Bigelow about Eagle Down on that visit," said Bob.

"No, that's not true."

"Well, we think you did. We are writing a story for tomorrow's paper, and that information will be in the article. Would you like to comment?"

"God! Don't put that in the paper, please," Jerry Baldwin pleaded.

"Why not?"

"You could get me killed!"

"Why? Who would kill you?"

"I can't say."

"Then, Mr. Baldwin, we have no choice but to put that information in the paper."

"No! I told you I would be murdered if that information was made public."

"Again, Mr. Baldwin, who would murder you?"

"I told you, I can't say. If I told you I was the one who told Harry about Eagle Down, would you keep it out of the paper?"

Carol jumped into the conversation. "Then there is a project called Eagle Down?"

"Yes!"

"What is the project about?"

"I'm sorry, but I cannot divulge that. I would be a dead man tomorrow. I have a family to think about. Now please don't print any of this. And don't contact me again. I don't want anyone to see me talking to you. Good night!"

He slammed the door. Carol looked at Bob. "Well, now we know there is a project called Eagle Down."

"Yeah, but how do we find out what's in it that people get murdered over it?"

* * *

When they left, the black Mercedes followed them. While the man was driving, he called his contact, who had a cell phone whose number was only given to the killer, so when his phone rang, he knew who it was. After two rings, a voice answered. "Yes?"

"The two reporters went to see Baldwin at his house. They had a lively conversation, and Baldwin was upset."

"Okay, take him out before he talks."

"Consider it done."

* * *

Back at the paper's headquarters, in Sam's office, Bob was explaining what they found out from Jerry Baldwin. "Now, Chief, we know there is a project called Eagle Down. But that's all we know. Baldwin knows what the project is about but says if he divulges it, he would be murdered."

"Murdered? The United States government does not go around murdering its citizens. If they commit sabotage, treason, or even murder, they get a trial. They just don't take them out and shoot them. There is something very sinister about this. I smell a big story here."

"Maybe Eagle Down isn't a government project," said Carol.

"Then what is it? It's in the majority leader's office, and one of his aides knows about it. Maybe they all do and are not talking. Okay, keep digging. So far, you have established that there is a project. You connected the two murders, and we know in both murders that this Eagle Down is involved."

Back at their desks, both were thinking, *How can we find out what that project is about?*

* * *

In another part of the world, a small country called Afastan was having a political uprising. Shaw Abbuldol was the leader. He was an extremely unpopular dictator. The population was hungry. They were going without food, and many were dying from starvation while Abbuldol was living a lavish lifestyle. Abbuldol ruled with an iron fist, and he had the military to back him up. The People's Party was up in arms. The recent election was rigged in favor of Abbuldol, and the People's Party protested in the streets with demonstrations. But the military put down all the protests and arrested many of the people. They had a quick trial and were promptly shot. The People's Party saw Abbuldol had to go from power, but the military was too strong to overcome with a revolt. In addition, the military was loyal to Abbuldol. The only way Abbuldol could be removed was by assassination.

The leaders of the People's Party sought out a professional killer. There was such a man. He was called the Ghost. His specialty was assassinating leaders. He demanded a high price for his assassinations, was a wanted man in many of the European countries, and was high on the wanted list of Interpol. He eluded all efforts to capture him. One reason was no one had a picture or fingerprints of the man. He was unknown to the CIA in the United States; he had never been in the United States. He traveled with several forged passports under different names.

The People's Party leader in Afastan knew of the Ghost and his reputation and spent months trying to locate him. He finally made contact through an ally of the Ghost in Cairo. After many negotiations, the party leader traveled to Cairo to meet the Ghost.

The Ghost was not a tall man, at just five feet ten inches. He was of Arab descent, he had olive-tinted skin and black hair, and his eyes were almost a piercing black. When the party leader met the Ghost, he was blindfolded to protect the Ghost's appearance. After a long discussion, it was agreed the party leader would transfer one million US dollars to a bank account in Switzerland and one million to be paid after the assassination.

The party leader was not told when the assassination would take place or how it would be accomplished, but the assassin said it would take place within two months. If the party leader changed his mind before the assassination, then the Ghost would keep the one million dollars up-front money.

When the assassination was carried out, the world papers carried the assassination of Abbuldol. No mention was made of the killer since no one had any idea who was responsible. The military police had no clue who the killer was. After the assassination, the Ghost slipped out of the country back to Cairo, with his second one million dollars deposited in his Swiss bank account.

* * *

Jerry Baldwin finished work in the evening and left to go to the parking garage where he kept his car. He lived in Falls Church, a small town twelve miles from Washington, DC, and would travel over the Francis Scott Key Bridge to get to work and travel home. It was getting dark, and when he pulled out of the garage, he didn't notice a black Mercedes following him. When he reached the bridge, traffic was light, and he was in the lane closest to the railing. As he traversed the bridge and got to the middle, the Mercedes pulled out from behind him and alongside him. Then the Mercedes' passenger window went down, and a shot was fired from the Mercedes into the vehicle driven by Jerry. The bullet didn't shatter the window glass but made a neat hole. But the bullet missed Jerry. It went right in front of his face. He looked over to the Mercedes and saw the sinister figure pointing a gun at him. It terrified him. He realized he was being assassinated. Before a second shot was fired, Jerry jammed on the accelerator of his car and sped away, with the Mercedes pulling in behind him. The two cars raced in and out of their lanes. Jerry was scared to death; he drove through traffic as fast as he could, considering the evening traffic.

He kept saying out loud in a quivering voice, "God, help me. Help me. God, help me." When traffic cleared, Jerry pushed down on the accelerator and reached speeds of eighty miles an hour, but the Mercedes kept right behind him. When there was no oncoming traffic, the Mercedes pulled up alongside Jerry's car and fired two more shots. One hit Jerry in his shoulder, and the other his face.

Jerry lost control of his car. It careened off the highway into a field, rolled over several times, and came to rest on its roof. The Mercedes roared away. But Jerry was not killed by the accident. A car following the two cars saw Jerry's car go off the highway and roll over, and the driver called 911 and reported the accident. In ten minutes, the State police and paramedics were on the scene. They removed Jerry from the car and took him to the hospital.

* * *

The following morning, Carol was reading the *Washington Post* and came across an article on page 2 with this lead headline: SENATOR'S AIDE SHOT. As she read the story, the name Jerry Baldwin jumped out at her. She quickly read the story then said to Bob, "I think Jerry Baldwin was right. Look at this article. Baldwin was shot last night on his way home. Three bullets were fired into his car. One hit him in the shoulder, and the third hit him in the face. His car went off the highway and rolled over."

"Damn it! He had reason to be scared. Did the article say he would live?"

"No. It just said he was in stable condition."

"Let's get to the hospital and see if he will talk to us now."

* * *

When they reached the hospital, they found his room. When they went in, a nurse was adjusting an intravenous drip. Carol asked the nurse, "How is he?"

She shook her head and said, "Not too good. He's in a coma."

"What's wrong with him? Will he be able to talk soon?"

"Can't tell. The doctor says he has a fractured skull as well as the wounds to his face and arm. He may come out of the coma in a day, or it may take a week or longer. Are you relatives?"

"No. We are reporters from the *Washington Ledger*. We wanted to interview him about his shooting."

"Well, he won't be ready to talk for at least a day. Call the front desk before you come out again. They will tell you if he's out of the coma."

As they were leaving the hospital, they passed a sinister-looking man. Carol turned to Bob and commented, "Did you see that man that just passed us? He looked so evil. He looked like pictures I saw of the devil, except he didn't have horns."

"Carol, you can't judge a man by his looks. He could be the kindest man in the world coming to visit his grandchildren."

"Of course you're right. But he looked evil."

The killer, whom Carol saw, went to the reception desk and inquired what room Jerry Baldwin was in. He went to the intensive care unit and into Jerry's room and saw Jerry was still alive. The nurse told him Jerry was in a coma and could be in it for days.

"Will he live?" the killer asked.

"Can't tell. If he survives the fractured skull, his other wounds are not life-threatening. He should make it."

"Thank you, nurse." He left the room.

As he walked down the hall, he looked for a doctor who had his hospital badge pinned on his blouse. He saw one coming, talking to a nurse. He purposely bumped into the doctor, and as he did, he lifted the doctor's plastic badge from his blouse. He did it so deftly the doctor was unaware the killer removed it from his blouse.

"Oh, excuse me, Doctor. How clumsy of me."

"That's okay," replied the doctor, smiling.

He put the hospital badge into his pocket and left. Then he went to a medical supply store and bought a set of hospital scrubs and white sneakers. He went to his apartment, put the scrubs on, and pinned the hospital badge to his blouse. Now he could walk the halls of the hospital with impunity. Then he tucked his Glock 17 pistol with a silencer behind in his waistband. Then he drove to the hospital.

When he reached the hospital, he went in and went directly to the intensive care unit. He walked slowly, taking care no one saw him go into Jerry's room. He paused just outside the room, looking up and down the hall to see if anyone was coming either way. When no one was in sight, he quickly slipped into the room. Jerry was lying unconscious, with a breathing tube in his mouth. The killer took out his pistol, pulled the pillow out from under Jerry's head, put it over his face, put the pistol to Jerry's forehead, and fired. With the silencer and the muzzle in the pillow, there was hardly any noise from the gunshot. He removed the pillow and saw the bullet hole in Jerry's head. He then put the pillow back under Jerry's head and turned his head away from the entrance door to his room. That way, a nurse just looking in would not see Jerry had been shot. He needed five minutes to get out of the hospital and into his car.

One nurse's aide saw him leave.

Half an hour later, a nurse went into Jerry's room to check on his vitals, and as she went to take his blood pressure, she saw the bullet hole in his forehead. She jolted back, let out a loud scream, and ran out of the room.

The hospital phoned the police about the murder, and twenty minutes later, two detectives from homicide came into Jerry's room and inspected Jerry's wound. One of the detectives said, "One shot to the head. Killed him instantly. Let's find out who this guy is."

They went to the floor desk and asked for the head nurse. "Nurse, I want to talk to everyone who was on this floor for the past hour. Get them here. Also get me this man's name and his next of kin."

No one recalled anything unusual, just doctors and nurses on the floor. One nurse's aide told the detectives, "I saw one doctor that I have never seen before in the hall. That's the only one I've seen other than the regular staff."

"What did this doctor look like?"

"He was tall, dark hair, a thin face, and a thin black mustache with a goatee."

"Sounds like Satan," he said, smiling.

The nurse responded, "Come to think of it, he did look like Satan."

"How do you know he was a doctor?"

"He wore a doctor's scrubs."

"Okay, my partner here will accompany you. I want you to go to every floor in this hospital and look in every room to see if you can see this doctor. If not, I would like you to go to our precinct and see a sketch artist and have him draw a likeness of this doctor for us."

* * *

At the precinct, the sketch artist finished his drawing based on the nurse's aide's description. He showed her the completed composite.

"Yes, that looks like him, even the long face. My, he does look like the devil, doesn't he?"

* * *

That afternoon, Sam was in his office, with the television on, listening to the network newscast, when another newsman came on the screen. "We had a special bulletin just in. Jerry Baldwin, an aide to Senator Saxton, the senate majority leader, was murdered today in Saint Paul's hospital. He was shot with a single bullet to the head while recuperating from an automobile accident and attempted murder that occurred yesterday while he was driving home from the Senate office building. The police have one suspect. Here's an artist's sketch of a man seen in the hall near Mr. Baldwin's room." The sketch of the killer was flashed on the screen. "He leaves a wife and two children. He has been an aide for five years."

Sam turned off the television and phoned Carol on his intercom. "Yes?" Carol answered.

"Get your tail in here, and tell Bob to come also! Pronto!" Sam growled.

Carol said to Bob, "The chief wants us. He sounded upset." When they came into his office, Sam was sitting in his chair, with his hand on his chin and his elbow on the arm of his swivel chair, like he was in deep thought.

"What's up, Chief?" asked Bob.

"Your key guy, that Baldwin fellow, who got shot last night."

"Yeah, what about him?"

"He was murdered today in the hospital. How's that strike you?"

"God Almighty!" said Carol. "Somebody wants to keep the Eagle Down story from coming out awfully bad. That's four people murdered to keep it under wraps."

"So now that the one lead you had is gone, what next? I tell you, this is one big story. We have to get our hands around this Eagle Down and see what it's about."

"I don't know where to turn, Chief," said Bob. "Baldwin was our only lead. With him gone, we have nothing."

"The TV news broadcast had a composite on the air of a suspect. Get ahold of that. We can use it in our story. Maybe someone might recognize the guy, if he is the killer. Carol, call your FBI friend. Tell him what you found out from Jerry Baldwin. Maybe that might give the FBI something to work with. And keep digging."

Carol called Dan Morris. "Hello, Agent Morris here," he answered.

"Dan, this is Carol. I need to talk to you."

"About what? The Eagle Down caper?"

"Yes, but much more."

"Okay. Where are you?"

"At the paper."

"All right, I'll be over in half an hour."

Carol put down the phone and said to Bob, "Dan's coming over."

"Good. Maybe he has something on Jerry's murder."

When Dan arrived, he went to the cafeteria with Carol and Bob. "Now what's this about the Eagle Down caper? Have you got something new?" Dan asked.

"Yes. Bob and I interviewed all the aides in Senator Saxton's office."

"About what?"

"The Eagle Down story."

"Carol, we interviewed all those people also concerning the Bigelow murders. We got nothing."

"Well, Bob and I did."

Surprised, Dan asked, "What did you get?"

"One of the senator's aides, Jerry Baldwin, confirmed that the information Patricia Manning gave us came from the Senator's office, which confirms her story. Baldwin would not tell us what Eagle Down was about but said his life was in danger and asked us to keep away from him."

"And now he's dead!"

"Yes, but there were two attempts on his life. Dan, whatever that Eagle Down is about must be horrendous to have four people killed over it."

"It sure looks that way. Not only that, Senator Saxton has lied to the FBI. Did Baldwin implicate Admiral Goodman?"

"No. We never asked him."

"I wonder if Baldwin was murdered just because he knew of Eagle Down or if he had some documents concerning the caper, just like Patricia Manning."

"Do you think he would keep it at home if he had it?"

"Maybe, but for something that secret, he could have used a safe-deposit box."

"That's it, Dan. I remember Patricia said her folder was in a safe-deposit box. Why don't we ask the banks if they have her as a safe deposit customer?"

"Carol, banks don't give out information like that on customers."

"Well, couldn't you get a warrant?"

"For which bank? All the banks in DC and all the banks in her hometown? No, Carol. No judge will sign a carte blanche warrant to search the records of all those banks. If we knew where she banked, that might help."

Carol then asked, "Did you see the composite of the murder suspect that was on the news?"

"Yes."

"Anything in the FBI files like him?"

"No. He's a strange-looking fellow."

"You know, when Bob and I went to see Baldwin in the hospital, I saw that man. I'm sure of it."

"You went to see Baldwin in the hospital?"

"Yes. We thought, after an attempt was made on his life, he might want to tell us more about Eagle Down."

"Did he tell you anything more?"

"No. He was in a coma"

"You know, Carol, the FBI is not involved in the Patricia Manning murder and this Baldwin murder. But if you uncover something that links them together, we will get involved with all the murders."

"Well, isn't Eagle Down enough of a link?"

"No. That's supposition, not even circumstantial. I agree, there appears to be a link, but we can't prove it."

"Dan, I would think four murders with the taint of this Eagle Down would be enough for you fellows to get involved."

"Carol, the FBI does not solve murder cases. That's for the local authorities. The only reason we got involved in the Bigelow murders is because the president asked the director to. And you know, I might add, watch yourself. If you dig up something about this Eagle Down, you may become a target too."

* * *

Several days later, Jerry Baldwin was laid to rest. Bob and Carol attended the graveside ceremony to see who attended the service. No one even resembled the killer. Another dead end.

On the way back to the paper's office, Carol said to Bob, "We might want to talk to Baldwin's wife. She might know something and not realize how important it is, like Jerry having a safe-deposit box."

"Yeah, but let's wait for a few days until she's over her initial grief."

* * *

Dan went back to the FBI building and asked to see the director. He was given an appointment. At the appropriate time, he went to the director's office. When he walked in, Clive Banner asked him to sit down. "What's on your mind, Dan?"

"You remember the two reporters I brought in to see you a while back? Carol Williams and Bob Grant?"

"Yes, I remember them. What about them?"

"They have been trying to get to the bottom of the story on Eagle Down."

"That again?"

"Yes, and they have done a pretty good job uncovering some facts or, should I say, coincidences."

"What kind of coincidences?"

"Things that seem to be related to this Eagle Down thing. You, of course, are aware of the Bigelow murders and the unexplained e-mail from Bigelow to Saxton and Goodman."

"Yes."

"Then there was the murder of Patricia Manning and her alleged holding of a folder on Eagle Down, which no one ever found, unless the killer found it."

"Yes, go on."

"Now they claim that Jerry Baldwin told them that there is a file on Eagle Down and Patricia Manning got the file from the senator's office. They went to see him in his office and then at his home. Right after that, someone tried to kill him, shooting him in his car. But that didn't kill him. So someone went into his hospital room and shot him."

"So they are assuming anyone who had knowledge of this Eagle Down was murdered to keep them quiet?"

"Yes, that's their conclusion."

"And what do you think, Dan?"

"It seems to make sense."

"So what do you propose?"

"Put me on the case. I can work with the local police. It might just solve the Bigelow murders. I'm sure your boss, the president, will be happy with that *and* we might find out what this Eagle Down thing is."

"Okay, Dan, have at it. But keep me apprised of anything you find."

CHAPTER 4

Clive Banner called the president and asked for a meeting, which was granted. When he arrived and was seated in the oval office, the president asked, "Why did you want to see me, Clive?"

"To give you an update on the Bigelow murders."

"Great. Do you have a suspect?"

"No, sir, but other factors have entered the investigation."

Harrison asked, appearing to be confused, "I don't understand what you mean."

"There have been other murders that we think are connected to the Bigelow murders."

"You mean other officials?"

"No. But a woman in George Saxton's office and one of his aides."

"If you mean Jerry Baldwin, I've read about him. Was the other murder that woman in Chantilly that the *Washington Ledger* connected to the Bigelow murders?"

"Yes."

"How are they connected, Clive?"

"Do you recall that Harry Bigelow sent an e-mail to Saxton and Goodman the day he was murdered?"

"Yes, but what's that got to do with this woman in Chantilly and this Baldwin fellow?"

"In that e-mail, Bigelow inquired about a program or bill called Eagle Down."

"Yes, I recall that."

"When the *Washington Ledger* wrote about that program, they asked anyone who had knowledge to come forward and call the paper or us, the FBI. Well, that woman, Patricia Manning, called the paper and said she had a folder with all the details of that program. That night, she was murdered, and her apartment was torn apart. We think the killer was after the folder."

"And Baldwin?"

"Two reporters from the paper got him to admit that there was such a program. Then he was shot, and his car was run off the road. He didn't die in the accident, but the next day, he was murdered in his hospital bed."

"So this program, Eagle Down, figures in some way with all four murders."

"Yes. It looks that way. One thing more, I questioned Saxton about that program, and he vehemently denied any knowledge of the program. And so did Admiral Goodman. It seems reasonable that if a woman in Saxton's office and one of his aides knew of the project, then Saxton surely must have known about it. But I can't figure out why he would deny it. He knows it's a felony to lie to our agency."

"So where does that leave the investigation?"

"I've assigned Dan Morris to all the murder cases, to follow up not only on the Bigelow murders but also on the other two and to get to the bottom of this Eagle Down mystery."

"Anything more, Clive?" the president asked.

"No, sir, but if I get anything new, I'll let you know."

When Banner left, the president called Paul Barrows into his office and informed him of what Clive Banner had to say.

"Then, Mr. President, the FBI is no closer to solving Harry's murder."

"True, but give them time."

* * *

Dan Morris called Carol and asked her to meet with him and to bring Bob along. They met in the newspaper's cafeteria.

"Carol, I want to tell you that the director has given me the case dealing with Eagle Down. That means all the murders connected to this program. I've thought about it and have come to the conclusion that the only way to solve these murders is to find out what is it about the program that ties all the murders together. I'm telling you this because I want you to work with me. Your paper could be a big asset as we get information on Eagle Down."

"Then you aren't going to pursue the killer?"

"Well, yes and no. I believe the killer is a professional. The first two murders were committed with the same gun. After you printed the story and revealed that bit of information, the third murder was committed with a different gun. I had our ballistics lab check out the slugs taken from Baldwin. The slug taken from his shoulder from the shooting in the car and the slug taken from his head are from the same weapon. This guy is clever. You saw him in the hospital. You put the composite picture in the paper, and I put it on the ten most-wanted list."

"Dan, he had a very distinctive look. He shouldn't be hard to spot."

"Well, he could easily change his appearance: shave his mustache and beard, color his hair blond, wear dark-rimmed glasses, and other things. Besides, unless anything else turns up on Eagle Down, he may never need to come out in the open."

"So where do we go from here?"

"Talk to Baldwin's wife. See if her husband ever mentioned Eagle Down. Did he have any secret folders or a safe-deposit box? Like I said, pursue the program, not the murders."

* * *

Dan called Mrs. Baldwin and asked to come and talk to her. He invited Carol and Bob along. It had been several days since the funeral, and when Mrs. Baldwin answered the door, she was still dressed in a black dress in keeping with the mourning tradition.

"Mrs. Baldwin, I'm Agent Morris from the FBI. I called earlier."

"Yes, Mr. Morris, come in." She led them to the living room and invited them to sit down.

"Mrs. Baldwin," Dan said, "this is Ms. Williams and Mr. Grant. They are reporters for the *Washington Ledger*. They are following your husband's murder with me. I hope you don't mind talking in front of them."

"No, not at all. What can I do for the FBI, Mr. Morris?" she responded.

"Your husband had knowledge of a secret project that was in the majority leader's office. Very few people knew about the project, but your husband did."

"A secret project? Jerry never mentioned anything about a secret project—at least not that I recall."

"Did Mr. Baldwin ever mention the phrase Eagle Down?"

"No . . . not that I recall."

"Do you have a safe in the house?"

"No. Jerry had a safe-deposit box in town. That's where he kept all the important papers, like the insurance policy on the house and the kids' birth certificates. Things like that."

"Did Mr. Baldwin have a desk here in the house?"

"Yes, in the study. Why do you ask?"

"Mrs. Baldwin, would you mind if I went through his desk?"

Mrs. Baldwin said, "What are you looking for, Mr. Morris?"

"Some information on that secret project."

"Will it help find Jerry's killer?"

"I believe if we found out about that secret project, it would lead us to the killer."

"Then by all means, come with me to the study."

Mrs. Baldwin led them to the study, and she said, "There it is, just as Jerry left it. He was a lawyer, you know, and kept all his important papers in that desk or in his metal file. Feel free to look at everything. Call me when you are finished."

"Thank you, Mrs. Baldwin," Dan said. Then he turned to the other two. "Okay, Carol, you and Bob go through the desk. Look at every scrap of paper. Don't miss a thing. I'll go through his metal file."

For almost forty minutes, they looked at every piece of paper in the desk and in the metal file. Finally, Dan said, "Well, nothing here even suggests a secret project. Let's talk to Mrs. Baldwin again."

Dan went to the living room, where Mrs. Baldwin was sitting. She looked up and said, "Did you find anything that could help, Mr. Morris?"

"No. And we scrutinized every scrap of paper but found nothing."

"That's too bad. I was hoping Jerry left a clue for you."

"A clue? Was Mr. Baldwin concerned about something?"

"Oh yes. Ever since Mr. Bigelow and his wife were killed, he seemed jumpy and nervous."

"Did he say anything to you?"

"When I asked him why he was so irritable, he said it was just pressure at work."

"I'm going to ask you to do one more thing for me, Mrs. Baldwin. It's just a minor inconvenience."

"What's that?"

"Would you mind going to your bank and opening your safe-deposit box?"

"No. If you think Jerry might have put something in it about that secret project you talked about."

"That's precisely what I'm thinking, Mrs. Baldwin."

"All right. Let me get the key to the box and my purse."

They drove down to the Midtown Bank and went to the safe-deposit vault. Mrs. Baldwin signed in and retrieved the box and took it to a small cubicle. Dan and Mrs. Baldwin went through the entire contents of the box and found nothing but the Baldwins' personal papers. They took Mrs. Baldwin home and went back to the paper's office. On the way, Carol asked Dan, "So what's next, Sherlock?"

"The only other one to see the Eagle Down papers was Patricia Manning."

"Yeah, well, she isn't talking from her grave."

"No, but we never searched her apartment. We took the word of the detective that the papers were not there. We should go there and look at every possible hiding place she could have kept that folder in. Remember, those papers are the key to the murders. We have to find them if we are going to solve this case."

*　*　*

When they returned to the office, Sam called Bob and Carol into his private office. "Anything new on the murders for the afternoon edition?"

"Nope. The FBI director, Clive Banner, assigned Dan Morris to spend full-time on the case. We went to see Jerry Baldwin's widow. She let us look at his home file, and we went to his bank and looked in his safe-deposit box. But we got nothing."

"So what's next?"

"Dan Morris feels we should pursue the file on Eagle Down rather than the murderer. He says the file will tell us who the murderer is."

"Do you believe that?"

"It makes sense. Trying to find a man that looks like Satan when he can change his appearance is trying to find a pebble in a rock pile."

"Okay. Work with Dan but get me something to print," Sam ordered.

*　*　*

The next morning, Dan phoned Detective Gary Wilson in Chantilly. When Detective Wilson answered, Dan said, "Detective, this is Agent Dan Morris of the FBI."

"Yes, Agent Morris, what can I do for you? I thought you were through with our murder case."

"No. We are still pursuing the murderer, but more importantly, what the murderer was after."

"Oh, still looking for that folder, are you?"

"Yes. Is the apartment still sealed?"

"No. We released it a couple of days ago. If you want to get in, see the manager. You might be out of luck. He could have cleaned up the apartment by now."

"Well, I'll take my chances on that. I'm coming down."

"Suit yourself. The manager is in unit 1-A."

"Thanks, Detective. I'm the investigating agent on this case. If I get anything new, I'll let you know."

"Thanks, Morris."

Dan called Carol. "Hi, this is Dan. I'm going down to Chantilly to search Patricia's apartment. Do you or Bob want to go along?"

"Just a minute, Dan." Carol asked Bob if he wanted to go, and he declined. Then she said, "Okay, Dan, I'll go with you. Bob said he has an article to finish for the afternoon edition. Pick me up out front in fifteen minutes."

On the way driving down to Chantilly, Carol asked, "Do you really think we will find that folder in the apartment? Remember, I told you Patricia said the folder was in the safe-deposit box in her bank."

"True. But she could have gotten it out before she went home that night. I just want to eliminate the possibility that it's there."

"Okay, but I doubt she went to a bank, took out that folder, and went back to her office with it. She was too frightened to have it in the first place. The bank would have been closed when she left work, so she couldn't have gotten it just before she went home."

"All a possibility, but let's make sure."

When they arrived at the apartment, they had the manager open the door. As Dan stepped in the apartment, he said to the manager, "From the looks of it, nothing has been cleaned up."

"That's right, Mr. Morris. I'm trying to locate Ms. Patricia's next of kin. All this furniture is hers as well as all the clothes. All I did was repair the door and the lock," the manager responded.

"That's all, sir. You can go. When we leave, I will lock the door." Turning to Carol, Dan said, "I'll start in the bedroom. You start in the kitchen. Look in everything, even behind the refrigerator, in the freezer, in pots with lids. Feel along the shelves. If the folder is flat, it could just be lying on the shelf."

Dan went into the bedroom. Starting in the closet, he felt along the shelf. He took all the clothes on the floor and placed them back in the closet, inspecting every garment. Next, he went to the dresser, pulled out the drawers, and looked on the bottom to make sure nothing was taped to it. As he put garments into the drawers, he felt every one. Then he took the mattress off the bed. Satisfied he had looked at every possible hiding place in the bedroom, he went to the living room. He first looked under all the furniture then looked on top of the china closet and in and under all the drawers. Carol finished her inspection in the kitchen and joined Dan in the search of the living room. When they finished, they sat down.

"I guess there is no folder in this apartment," Dan said, exasperated.

"I didn't think we would find it here. Patricia said it was in her safe-deposit box. I guess we can give up on finding that folder."

"Maybe so. But there could be another folder someplace. Did Patricia say how she came to get ahold of that file?"

"No. She just said she saw it and copied it."

"It must contain something important, horrendous, or very secret for her to just make a copy of that file."

"Do you think it's a war plan?"

"No. If it were, it wouldn't be in Saxton's office. It would be in the Pentagon."

"Then what could it be about?"

"I have no idea. But it killed four people to keep it from going public. That much we know. Okay, we're through here. Let's go."

* * *

When Carol returned to the paper's headquarters, Sam called her and Bob into his office. "Anything new on Eagle Down?"

"No," said Carol. "I went with Dan Morris to Patricia Manning's apartment to search for the folder she said she had."

"Did you find anything at all?"

Carol said, "No, Chief."

"Well, we can't let this story die. You two write up a story for this afternoon's edition. Summarize what we know and write up that missing folder. Emphasize it in the article. Maybe we can stir something up."

* * *

The killer had shaved off his mustache, goatee, and head and put on heavy, dark-rimmed glasses. He no longer looked like the police artist's sketch. He had followed Dan and Carol to Chantilly and waited until they left then followed them back to the newspaper's office. Several hours after the afternoon edition of the *Washington Ledger* hit the street, the cell phone of the killer rang. He answered. "Yeah?"

"Those two reporters are getting too close. See if you can put them in the hospital and keep them there for a while. I think our plan may be put into effect soon. Then I don't care what they find out. Can do?"

"Can do! An automobile accident would work."

"Don't kill them. That would put too much heat on the cops to dig into the accident."

"Don't worry. I can handle it."

* * *

Both Carol and Bob lived in the town of Falls Church, about ten miles from Washington, DC. They traveled back and forth to work together, trading cars each week. This week, it was Bob's turn to drive. When they left the parking garage, it was dusk. As soon as they turned onto the street, a black Mercedes pulled away from the curb and followed them. They went over the Francis Scott Key Bridge into Virginia. They were on the highway and talking about the article they wrote that day. Bob was going fifty miles an hour, with the Mercedes coming up from behind. When the Mercedes was within twenty feet of Bob's car, the killer jammed the accelerator down to the floorboard and rammed the back of Bob's car, causing a loud bang. This caused Bob's car to leap forward and sent Bob and Carol back against their seats.

"Jesus Christ! What was that?" Bob shouted as he looked into the rearview mirror. The Mercedes backed off and then went forward again, slamming into Bob's rear end.

Bob's face turned white; he was frightened. Carol turned and looked as the Mercedes came at them a third time.

"He's going to ram us again!" said Carol in a hysterical voice.

The Mercedes hit them a third time, and Bob almost lost control of his car. Bob pressed down on the accelerator to get away from the Mercedes, and as he sped up, the Mercedes followed suit. Both cars were racing down the highway at seventy miles an hour, weaving in and out of traffic.

Carol looked behind and shouted, "He's following us!"

Bob pushed harder on the accelerator, and the car was now racing at ninety miles an hour, with the Mercedes close behind. The speeding cars went in and out of traffic, with Bob blowing his horn to get traffic out of his way. Down the highway they went at high speed. The Mercedes pulled up alongside Bob's car and turned his steering wheel to the right. The side of the Mercedes slammed into Bob's car. It pushed his car to the dirt on the roadside. Bob almost lost control but managed to get the car back on the pavement. The Mercedes slammed into Bob's car again. This time, Bob lost control, and his car went off the road. Carol screamed as the car bounced over a ditch into a field at high speed and rolled over five times—first side to side then end over end—and came to rest upside down, raising a big cloud of dust and dirt.

The killer watched Bob's car roll over again and again. He smiled, pleased he had done the right amount of damage, and continued down the highway at high speed to get away.

Several cars behind Bob's car saw his car go off the highway and stopped to see if they could help. They raced over to the upside-down car and looked in. Bob was unconscious, still strapped into his seatbelt, arms hanging down. Carol was half-conscious and moaning. The windshield had shattered and sent pieces of glass into her face and scalp, so she was bleeding. One of the drivers called 911 on his cell phone.

One man lay on the ground next to Carol, who was upside down and still strapped in the seat by her seat belt. The man asked her, "Are you okay, miss?"

Carol could hear the man's voice but didn't understand what he was saying. She just kept moaning. Another man came around to look into the car and saw Carol. He said, "We ought to get them out of the car. It could catch fire."

The other man said, "No. If they are injured, we will only make their injuries worse."

The man lying on the ground next to Carol kept talking to her to keep her awake.

A siren was heard wailing in the distance. Then a second siren was heard. Soon, the firemen and police arrived. They took Bob and Carol to the hospital emergency room, where two doctors examined them. Carol was awake. Her injuries were minor. She had cuts on her face and arms, and her right arm was broken.

After x-rays were taken, it was determined Bob had a severe concussion from his head slamming into the pillar between the two car doors. Bob was sent to the ICU, and Carol was put into a regular room for the night.

* * *

The next morning, Carol awoke and asked for her cell phone. She dialed Sam's number, but he was not in the office yet. She left a message for him to call her. She said it was an emergency.

When Sam came into his office, he saw his message light blinking and listened to the message from Carol. He dialed her number. When Carol heard her cell phone ring, she answered it. "Hello?"

"Hello. Carol, is that you?"

"Yes, Sam."

"You left a message and said it was an emergency. What's wrong?"

"Sam, Bob and I are in a hospital."

"A hospital? What the hell are you doing there?"

"We were in a car accident! No, not an accident. We were run off the road by another car."

"How are you? Are you hurt bad?"

"I'm not. I just have some cuts and bruises and a broken arm. But Bob has a severe concussion. He's in the ICU."

"Jesus Christ! What hospital are you in?"

"Falls Church Memorial."

"Okay, I'll be right down."

He hung up the phone, grabbed his jacket, and said to his secretary as he ran out, "Bob and Carol were in a car accident. They are in Falls Church Memorial. I'm going there."

Sam stopped at the hospital receptionist and found out which room Carol was in and which room Bob was in. When he walked into Carol's room, she was dressed and putting on her shoes. Sam asked, "Are you allowed to get dressed?"

"Yes, Sam. The doctor released me. I was going to the ICU and see Bob. Now that you're here, we can go together."

"Wait a minute. On the phone, you said someone ran you off the road. Did you mean they did it deliberately?" Sam asked, only know grasping what Carol had said to him on the phone.

"Yes. Without a doubt."

"Tell me what happened."

"After Bob and I left the office and went over the Francis Scott Key Bridge, a few miles down the road, a black Mercedes ran into the back of Bob's car."

"Was that an accident?"

"No. He did it deliberately."

"How could you tell?"

"Because he did it two more times. Each time, he left a space between the cars then raced his car into ours. After that, he pulled alongside and pushed us off the road. Bob managed to get back on the road the first time, but the second time, we went into a ditch and rolled over and over. It was horrible. I thought I was going to die."

"How did you know it was a Mercedes?"

"It had that ornament on the front of the hood. You know, the kind Mercedes's have. It was a black Mercedes."

"Did the police get any description?"

"I don't know, Sam. Both Bob and I were out of it until we got to the hospital."

"Why would someone try to kill you?"

"Are you kidding? After all the articles in our paper about Eagle Down, someone thought we were getting too close."

"You're probably right. We need to get you and Bob some protection."

"Why? Do you think they will try again?"

"Carol, it doesn't take a genius to figure out. If they killed four people to keep this thing, this Eagle Down, from coming out in the open, they won't hesitate to go after you and Bob again if you are getting close. They want to shut you up."

"I guess you're right. I'm going to call Dan and tell him what happened, but first, let's go see Bob."

When they walked into Bob's room, he was already awake. He had several intravenous tubes going into his arm and oxygen going into his nose.

"Hi, Bob. Good, you're awake," said Carol.

"What happened, Carol? The last thing I remember was talking to you in the car. Then I woke up in this place."

"Don't you remember? A black Mercedes ran us off the road."

"No, I don't remember that."

"Bob, I think it was the killer who murdered four people over Eagle Down."

"Why would he kill us? We don't know anything."

"He doesn't know that. Maybe he thinks we know more than we do and wants to shut us up."

"God Almighty! That means he will try again."

"Maybe. But that makes it more imperative we find out about Eagle Down before he tries again."

Sam then said, "Maybe I should take you off this story. I don't want my two reporters murdered. Besides, with that broken right arm, you can't type your stories, and Bob will be laid up for a spell. Carol, take some time off and rest up."

* * *

The debate over the stimulus bill was still going on in the capitol. Neither the majority leader in the Senate nor the speaker in the House would bring the bill up for a vote. Both claimed there were not enough yes votes to pass the bill. The Senate needed sixty votes to pass the bill, and the House of Representatives needed only a simple majority. The editorials in the newspapers throughout the country were debating the bill also. They were arousing the people almost to riot. The people were confused by the negative television ads on both sides, not knowing which ad to believe.

Outside the capitol building, protesters were gathered for both sides of the issue. They carried signs, and on occasion, they would clash, requiring the police to intercede and break up the fighting parties. Some of the signs read "Don't mortgage my child's future" and "Keep our future debt-free." The opposition's signs read "Pass the bill, we need jobs" and "Save our economy, pass the bill." The police would move in and break up the melee with billy clubs and water pressure hoses and arrest some of the people fighting one another. All major cities in the country were having the same protests. The news media covered all these demonstrations, reporting them on the national evening news, causing the people to become upset over the debate and carry on the debate even in business offices.

The president called his cabinet into session. After everyone was seated, he said, "I've called you here because we have a serious problem on our hands. This debate is getting out of hand. It is not only Congress that's debating my stimulus bill but also the whole nation. Every major newspaper has editorials almost every day. Major networks on the evening news are not just reporting the news but also taking a position for or against my bill. Debates are the backbone of our democracy, but rioting and name-calling are not. People are pouring into the streets, demonstrating, and in some cases, riots are breaking out as the two sides clash. We have to get an up or down vote on this bill and put an end to this debate. It's tearing the country apart. Now, who has any ideas to bring this problem to a conclusion?"

The vice president, Grace Arden, said, "Sir, the only way this is going to get resolved is for Congress to vote on the bill. I don't doubt that if the bill is passed or voted down, there will be unhappy people out there. But at least that will calm the masses down and stop the debate."

"Okay, how do we do that? The majority leader in the Senate and the house speaker are the only ones who can bring the bill up for a vote. And they seem to be stuck in neutral."

"Use the power of your office. Get on national television. Get the people behind you. Tell them to e-mail or write to their congressmen and senators to bring the bill up for vote. Tell them to remind their representatives that midterm elections are only a year away."

"You think that will force Saxton and Giddings to bring the bill up for a vote?"

Almost everyone in his cabinet nodded. "Yes," said the vice president. "The first and most important thing these politicians think of is holding on to their seat. That is their highest priority."

"All right. I'll ask my news publicist to get with the networks and set up a time for the broadcast. Then I'll have my speech writers go to work. Now, on to other business."

* * *

Sam took Carol home and went back to his office. He wrote an article describing what happened to Carol and Bob and why they were attacked and again asked anyone with information about Eagle Down to come forward.

Carol called Dan at his office. "Dan, I called you to let you know Bob and I were attacked last night on our way home."

"Attacked? How?"

"We were rear-ended three times, so it was no accident. Then the son of a bitch sideswiped us twice, and we went end over end in the car off the road into a field."

"Good God Almighty! Are you or Bob hurt?'

"Bob's in the hospital with a severe concussion. I got a broken arm and some cuts and bruises."

"So it was on purpose."

"Yep. He kept after us until we crashed. I'll bet it was the killer. When he pulled up alongside us, I saw a man with a bald head, a long face, and glasses. I'll bet it's our killer disguising himself. If I saw him again, I would recognize him."

"Okay, let's pull out the artist's sketch and take off the hair on the head, take off the facial hair, and put on a pair of glasses. Then let's see if you can identify him."

"Dan, I have a broken arm. I can't drive with one hand. Can you pick me up?"

"Can do. Give me your address."

"Dan, it's the same apartment I was in when we were dating."

"Right! I'll pick you up in an hour."

* * *

Carol and Dan watched the sketch artist change the composite picture of the killer. "How's that?" he asked as he finished.

"Great, but make the rims on the eyeglasses darker and wider."

He touched up the composite. "How's that?" he said. "Perfect. That, Dan, is how our killer looks now. I would recognize him anywhere."

"Okay, I'll get this composite on the street and in all post offices and all federal buildings and send copies to every police precinct and sheriff's office for fifty miles around. You, young lady, get your editor to print this in today's edition of your paper."

"Can do if you drive me over there."

"Sorry, I forgot about your arm. Of course I'll drive you."

* * *

Later, Dan and Carol went to see Sam Corcoran. When they walked into his office, he looked up, surprised, took off his glasses, and laid them on his desk. "I thought you were going to take time off. And who is this guy?"

"This guy, as you call him, is Dan Morris, the special FBI agent assigned to the Bigelow murders."

"Oh, your ex, eh?"

Carol responded, "Yes, but he's letting us work with him. You know, Sam, that would give us an exclusive."

"Yeah, if he solves the case."

"I will," said Dan as he reached out and shook Sam's hand.

"So why are you here?" Sam asked.

"Last night, when the killer pulled up alongside our car, I looked over and saw the man driving the car. When he pulled up again, I got another look at him. So I could identify him if I saw him again," Carol said.

"Well, that's not very likely. I doubt he is just going to walk up to you and let you get a good look at him."

"No, Sam. Dan had the sketch artist at the FBI take the composite that the nurse at the hospital described to the police sketch artist and removed his hair on his head and facial hair and put on glasses. And it's a dead ringer for the man I saw last night. Take a look at this," she said as she handed him a copy.

He looked at it and commented, "I get it. You want me to print this with the story of your attack."

"Yes. And Dan is going to circulate it to all law enforcement agencies and federal buildings all around here. Someone is bound to spot him."

"Okay, done. That will add a little color to our story. Now, you get out of here and get some rest. By the way, how is Bob doing?"

"When I left, he was doing fine. When Dan drives me home, I'll stop in and see him."

Dan and Carol stopped at the hospital. Bob was awake and was feeling better.

"The doctor said I will have to stay here for a few days. My concussion should be better by then, at least enough for me to go home and rest. Now tell me what happened."

"It is my opinion and Dan's that the killer was after us because we were getting too close to finding out what Eagle Down was about."

"But, Carol, we have no idea what that's about."

"I know that, and you know that, but the killer doesn't. Anyway, last night, he rammed our car from behind three times at fifty miles an hour, then pulled up beside us and pushed our car off the road. We flipped a number of times. Both times, I got a good look at him. I know I was in a panic, but I saw him and won't soon forget what he looks like. Dan had the FBI artist alter the composite made by the

Georgetown police. This guy has shaved his head and face and now wears glasses. His new identity will be plastered all over our front page and in all federal buildings."

"Another thing, Bob, I'm having all the body shops around DC be on the lookout for a black Mercedes with damage to the front end and passenger side, just in case this guy wants to get his car fixed," said Dan.

"What about my car, Carol?"

"Forget it, Bob. It's a total loss."

Bob said, "Well, you'll have to drive when I get out of here."

"I can't, not with my arm in a sling. We use my car and you drive."

"Bob," Dan said, "I'm asking the Falls Church Police to put a guard outside your room."

"Why?"

"The killer tried to kill you and failed. He may try again. And you're vulnerable lying here in bed. Remember Jerry Baldwin?"

"Yeah, you're right."

* * *

Dan drove Carol to her apartment. As she got out of the car, she asked, "Would you like to come in and have some lunch?"

"Sure. Besides, I don't feel comfortable with you alone in your apartment. Bob may not be the only one at risk."

"The killer doesn't know where I live."

"Don't count on it. He followed you from the paper's office last night. He could have been following you for days."

"I never noticed anyone following me."

"If he was good at his job, you wouldn't see him."

* * *

That afternoon, when the *Washington Ledger* hit the street, the killer got a phone call. "I read the paper. I see one is in the hospital and one has a broken arm. Good work. That should keep them off the story for a while. I think it's time to get in touch with our friend in Cairo."

"Okay. I'll catch a plane tonight."

"Your likeness is in the paper. Can you use another disguise?"

"Yeah. I have a blond wig and mustache. That fits my other passport. With that and dark glasses, no one will recognize me."

"Okay. Call me from Cairo when you make contact."

"Will do."

* * *

That evening, the killer drove to Reagan National Airport, went to the ticket counter of British Airlines, and purchased an airline ticket for London then on to Cairo. The ticket clerk asked to see his passport, with which the killer obliged. The clerk checked the date and the photo on the passport and looked at the killer's face then handed back his passport. The flight left at midnight. Because of the time difference, the plane landed at Heathrow Airport in London late the next morning. Then he changed flights and took a flight to Cairo. He checked into a hotel, and when he was settled, he dialed a local phone number. The answer from the phone was in Arabic.

"Hello?"

The killer spoke Arabic. "I have come to enlist the aid of a mutual friend."

"Which friend?"

"One who takes care of annoying people."

"Where are these annoying people?"

"In America."

"How soon are these people to be taken care of?"

"Pretty quick."

"Our mutual friend is expensive."

"I'm aware of that. I am authorized to approve of his fee."

The man on the other line responded, "Come to your hotel lobby at ten sharp tomorrow morning. Wear a white handkerchief in the breast pocket of your jacket. There will be an Arab wearing a fez who will take you to a limo. There, you will be blindfolded and taken to our mutual friend."

"Agreed."

* * *

The next morning, the killer stood in the lobby, waiting for an Arab wearing a fez. A man came into the lobby wearing a fez. He stopped and looked around then saw the killer with his white handkerchief in his jacket breast pocket and walked up to him and asked in English, "Sir, are you waiting for a limo?"

"Yes, I am," said the killer.

"Then follow me."

Out at the curb was a black Cadillac limo with a driver. "Get in," said the Arab. The killer got in the limo, and the Arab went around to the other door and got in. Then he took a red cloth out of his coat pocket and said to the killer, "Bend over." Then he tied the red cloth around the killer's head, covering his eyes. Then he said to the driver, "Go."

The killer was going to ask a question of the Arab wearing the fez. As he started to speak, the Arab said, "Do not speak. You will talk to our friend when we get there."

For twenty minutes, the limo went through the streets of Cairo. Many times, the limo stopped, and the killer could hear the driver cursing and telling people to get their animals out of the road. Finally, the limo stopped, and the Arab got out. He grabbed the hand of the killer and led him out of the car. They walked up to a door and into a house. The killer was led through several rooms and was told to sit down on a wooden chair. His blindfold was removed by the Arab, and the Arab left. The killer looked around and saw he was in a room with little light. The only light was from a doorway that was partially open. All that was in the room was a wood table and another wood chair. He sat there for ten minutes. Then a man came into the room. It was so dark the face of the man was not distinguishable. He sat down and said, "You have need of my services?"

"Yes, if you are the one called the Ghost."

"I am."

"My employers in America have a need to eliminate certain parties."

"Are they government figures?"

"They are."

"Who are they?"

The killer pushed a piece of paper over the table to the Ghost, with two names on it. The Ghost read the names but said nothing for a few seconds. Then he said, "It will be expensive."

"My employers have authorized me to approve the sum."

"This will cost five million dollars, American money—half now and the other half when the contract is completed. I will give you a bank account number for a bank in Switzerland. You will wire-transfer the money to that account. When I learn the money is transferred, I will undertake the project. Understand, if, after you pay the first half, you decide to cancel the project, I keep the first half. Understood?"

"Understood. When will the project be completed?"

"I can't tell. First, get the money to my account. I will then start the project. How long it will take depends on the itinerary of the subjects. Tell me your name."

"I am called Hassan Kahil."

"Write down your address in the States. I will contact you when I arrive. I will need your help."

Hassan wrote down his Washington address and handed it to the Ghost.

"Now go," said the shadowy figure.

The Ghost got up and left. Hassan got up, and the Arab came into the room and blindfolded him again, led him out to the limo, and drove him back to the hotel. He flew back to the United States. When he got back to his room, he phoned his contact. "The arrangements are made," he said. "I will give you an account number of a bank in Switzerland to wire-transfer the money. The price is five million, half now and half when the contract is complete. If you cancel the project, he keeps the first half."

"Good work. I'll arrange for the money to be sent."

And Hassan hung up his cell phone.

CHAPTER 5

Carol made lunch with one arm in a sling as Dan watched in amazement. "You do pretty good with one hand there, lady."

"Thanks. It's ready. Sit down."

As they sat eating, Carol asked Dan, "Did the police in Chantilly ever tell you what they took as evidence from Patricia's apartment?"

"No. I never asked. Why?"

"I got to thinking, when we searched the apartment, we never found her purse."

"Come to think of it, you're right. I wonder if the killer took it. But why worry about her purse?"

"Well, in it, she would have her wallet, maybe a checkbook. We never ran across her checkbook. If we knew what bank she did business with, you could get a warrant to see if she had a safe-deposit box there."

"I guess I could," Dan said.

"Wait a minute. We never ran across a safe-deposit key in her apartment. I'll bet it's in her purse. I remember she said she was going to the bank to get the folder from her safe-deposit box. I bet she had the key in her purse."

"You could be right."

Carol then said, "Dan, phone Detective Wilson in Chantilly and see if they have her purse."

Dan took out the detective's card from his wallet, which had his phone number on it. Then he dialed the number. A voice said, "Detective Wilson here."

"Detective, this is Agent Morris. When I was down to see the apartment of Patricia Manning, I just realized we never saw her purse. Do you have it?"

"I don't know. Let me check the evidence room. I'll get back to you. Give me your number."

Twenty minutes later, Dan's phone rang. It was Detective Wilson. "Yes, Agent Morris, we have it. Is there some reason you want it? We were saving it for the next of kin."

Dan said, "Yes. Check and see if there is a checkbook in the purse."

The detective came right back. "Yes, there is."

"What bank?"

"Just a minute. Yeah, it's the First Bank of Virginia, here in Chantilly."

"Now check and see if there is a safe-deposit box key."

"Okay, hold on," Detective Wilson said, then he came back in a minute. "Yep, but it doesn't have a box number on it."

"That's okay. Now hold onto that purse. I'm going to a federal judge and getting a search warrant for that box. I'll be down tomorrow morning."

"Sure thing. Come and see me when you get here."

When Dan hung up, he shouted, "We found it, Carol! We found it!"

"What have you found?"

"The folder, the Eagle Down folder! It's in a bank safe-deposit box in Chantilly."

"Are you sure?"

"Well, it wasn't in her apartment. You said she said it was in a safe-deposit box. The box key is in her purse. The folder has to be there."

"So what do you do now? Go down and get it?"

"No. The bank will not allow me to just go in and open the box. I'll need a warrant from a judge. I'll have to get to the director and ask him to get the warrant."

"Can I go with you?"

"No, You stay here. When I get the warrant, I'll come by and pick you up. Then we'll go to Chantilly together."

* * *

Dan drove back to Washington, DC, to FBI headquarters. He asked to see the director. When Dan went into the director's office, Clive Banner invited him to sit down.

"What have you got for me, Dan?"

"Sir, I think I have found the Eagle Down folder that Patricia Manning had."

"You did? Where is it?"

"I don't have it in my possession. But I know where it is. In a safe-deposit box in a bank in Chantilly."

"Well, why didn't you get it?"

"As you know, the bank will not let me in the box without a search warrant or a court order."

"That's right."

"That's why I'm here. To ask for a warrant."

"Dan, I'll have our lawyers write up a warrant right away, and you can take it to Federal Judge Homer Garner. I'll call him and tell him you are coming. Go down to our legal department. I'll call ahead. Give them the name of the bank, the location, and what box you wish to investigate."

Dan waited for the legal department to type the warrant then took it to the federal judge, who signed it. Then he drove to Falls Church to pick up Carol. They drove to Chantilly. They went to the police precinct and picked up the safe-deposit box key from Detective Wilson then drove to the bank.

The manager of the First Bank of Virginia was Walter Peters, and when Carol and Dan entered the bank, they went directly to him.

Peters had a metal desk sign that read walter peters, manager. Dan walked up and said, "Mr. Peters."

"Yes?" he replied, looking up.

"I'm Agent Morris of the FBI, and this lady is Carol Williams. I have a federal warrant to take the contents of a safe-deposit box rented by a woman named Patricia Manning, one of your customers."

He handed the warrant to Peters, who read it then looked at Dan. "Yes, Ms. Manning was one of our customers. Such a tragic death. Do you have her key?"

"Yes."

"Fine. Follow me to the vault."

Peters picked up the common key that fit all safe-deposit boxes and looked in the file to see which box belonged to Patricia Manning. Then he went to the box. When it was opened, Dan looked in the box. There were several items in it, but sitting on top was a folded manila envelope. He took it out, opened it, and took out three sheets of paper. On the first page was a heading: eagle down project. He quickly went through the rest of the documents to determine that nothing else was related to the Eagle Down Project. He closed the box and thanked Peters. He and Carol went to the car.

As they sat in the car, Dan started to read the documents. As he read, he whistled and looked at Carol. When he was through reading it, he put down the documents and said to Carol, "Damn! No wonder four people were killed. What a horrendous plot!"

"Dan, what is it? Can I see it?"

"Carol, this document contains a plot that affects our country's national security. If I let you read it, you must promise me that you will not print it or tell anyone what you read. Is that understood?"

Carol thought for a moment then said, "Is it that important, Dan?"

"Yes, Carol. This has to be kept under wraps until the director of the FBI and the Secret Service director decide what to do."

"All right. You have my word."

He handed the document to Carol, who began to read it. After she read the first page, she turned to the second page and looked at Dan. "Wow, this is powerful stuff."

Dan just nodded. Carol read the rest of the document then looked at Dan. "I see what you mean. What are you going to do?"

"Take it to my boss and pronto. This plot could already be in progress."

They drove to the FBI building, and Dan asked for an emergency meeting with Clive Banner. Banner was in a staff meeting, and when his secretary told him of Dan's request, he stopped his meeting and asked his staff to leave. He then told his secretary to send Dan in. When Dan came in, Banner was surprised to see Carol with him.

"What's this emergency, Dan? And why is she here?"

"You remember Carol Williams, the reporter from the *Washington Ledger*?"

"Yes, but why is she here?"

"She's been working with me on the Bigelow case. She's the one that uncovered that Patricia Manning had a folder with the Eagle Down project."

"So?"

"We found the file in Patricia Manning's safe-deposit box, and Carol has seen it. I thought after you read it, you might want to have her in on the case and swear her to secrecy."

"Okay. What have you got?"

Dan handed the folder to Clive, who opened it and started to read. "Jesus Christ. Damn! Is this for real?" When he finished reading, he put the document down. He looked up at Dan. "Do you believe this?"

"Well, sir, four people have been murdered to keep it quiet."

"Yes, I guess you're right. I'll call Timothy Hendricks, head of the Secret Service, and get him over here."

He called his secretary on the intercom. "Ruth, get me Timothy Hendricks on the phone and three cups of coffee." He looked at Dan and Carol and inquired, "Black or with cream and sugar?"

Both said black.

Then Clive said to his secretary, "Make all three black."

In a minute, Clive's intercom buzzed. "Mr. Hendricks is on line 1, sir," his secretary said.

"Thank you." He pressed the button on his phone and said, "Tim, how you doing?"

"Fine, Clive. What's on your mind?"

"I have something here that was just uncovered. You need to see it."

"What's it about?"

"I'd rather not tell you over the telephone. Can you come over here right away? It's urgent."

"Sure. I can be there in fifteen minutes."

"I'll be waiting."

When he hung up, he asked Dan, "Tell me how you came to get this file, Dan."

Dan went through the whole story of Carol remembering she never saw a purse in the apartment and how they tracked it down. Then Clive's secretary brought in the coffee. While they were waiting for Timothy, Clive said to Carol, "You know, miss, now that you are in the loop, you cannot disclose anything you read or print anything that we discuss with the Secret Service."

"I understand, sir. But my boss, the editor, should know. I have an obligation to tell him. After all, he put me on the story."

"Well, let's wait until we discuss it with the Secret Service. Then we will decide who gets to know."

They sat waiting for Timothy Hendricks. Then Clive's intercom buzzed. "Yes?" he said after pushing the button.

The secretary said, "Mr. Hendricks is here, sir."

"Fine, send him in."

Hendricks came in, and Clive introduced him to Carol and Dan. Hendricks then asked, "Okay, Clive, what do you have that's so hush-hush?"

Clive handed him the document and said, "Here, read this."

Tim started reading and, on occasion, would look up at Clive and go on reading. When he finished, he said, "This must be a joke."

"I think it's real. Four people have been murdered to hide it."

"Clive, this is a plot to kill the president and vice president of the United States then put the speaker of the House as president and the majority leader of the Senate as vice president."

"Yes. And then kill the stimulus bill, which is the president's highest priority," replied Clive.

"So that's what this plot is about: the stimulus bill. I knew that it was a highly controversial bill, but in my wildest dreams, I never thought someone would kill the president and the vice president over it. Who's behind this, Clive?"

"I haven't the foggiest notion."

"And who is this Ghost?" Tim asked.

Clive responded with "Apparently, a hired assassin."

"I've never heard of him. Have you?"

"No. But he could be foreign. I can have the CIA check him out. They may have heard of him."

"Do that. Clive, I am going to treat this as a credible threat against the president and vice president. Are you going to start hunting for the planners of this plot and start looking for this Ghost?"

"Yes. Right away."

"The beneficiaries of this plot are Sam Giddings and George Saxton. Can they be behind it?"

"I have no way of knowing. When this first surfaced, I quizzed George on his knowledge of Eagle Down, but he pleaded ignorance. Same with Admiral Goodman."

"Admiral Goodman? What's he got to do with this?"

He was sent an e-mail from the assistant chief of staff of the president the day he was murdered, asking Saxton and Goodman if they knew anything about Eagle Down."

"And he denied any knowledge of the plot?"

"Yes. One thing puzzles me. Why is the plot called Eagle Down?"

"I can figure that out, Clive. The president, vice president, and anyone being guarded by the Secret Service are given a code name. So when we talk on the radio to one another about where the subject is or is going, we don't use the real name. The president's code name is Eagle. I suspect the phrase 'Eagle Down' means taking the president down. You see, the president's wife is Queenie, and their daughter is called Chic."

"So someone who has knowledge of these code names is behind this plot."

"Could be. But now that I think this threat is real, I am going to tell all my people on the president's and vice president's guard detail to be on the alert for anything unusual. By the way, where is the debate on that bill at the moment? This plot is to be carried out before the vote."

"I don't know, but we can find out"

"I best look at the president's calendar. I hope he isn't planning any trips that will be difficult to guard against."

"What about the vice president?"

"Well, she seldom leaves the White House, so she's easier to guard. But lately, she's been going on trips with the president." Tim then turned to Carol and said, "Ms. Williams, you realize your paper cannot print any of this. If any of this gets out, it will drive the conspirators deeper underground and will alert this Ghost fellow to be more careful. We need to let them think that their plot has not been uncovered. Understand?"

"Yes, I do. But can't you tell my editor? He won't print any of this if you explain it's a matter of national security. If you don't, he will be constantly after me to get more information on the murders and the phrase Eagle Down."

"Do you think we can trust him?" asked Tim.

"Yes. He's tough as an editor but a very honorable man. Besides, if you offer him an exclusive on the story, I doubt he will refuse."

"Fine, then let's go see him now."

* * *

Sam was sitting in his office, reading some of the articles that were to be in tomorrow's paper, when he looked up and saw Carol, Dan Morris, Clive Banner, and Timothy Hendricks walk into his office. His mouth dropped open as he saw these high officials come into his office. He jumped out of his chair and said, "Jesus Christ, Carol! What have you done to bring the head of the FBI, the head of the Secret Service, and an FBI agent in here?"

"Calm down, Chief. There is no problem. Dan and I found the document on the 'Eagle Down' phrase."

"It took all this muscle to find it?"

"No. I'll let Mr. Banner explain."

"Okay, all of you, sit down and explain it to me," replied Sam.

"Mr. Corcoran, what I have to tell you has to be kept secret. You cannot print it or tell anyone about it," said Banner.

Sam asked, "Is it a big story?"

"Yes. Probably the biggest in your career."

"And I can't print it?"

"That's right. Not until the whole story unfolds. You will be given an exclusive."

"Well, now, that sounds better."

"This is not a trivial matter, Mr. Corcoran. It concerns national security. I must have your word that nothing I tell you will leak out to the public. Will you give me your word?" Mr. Banner said.

"Yes! When will I know I can print it?"

"We will tell you, although when you hear what this is about, you will realize that you will know it's over without anyone telling you. We, of course, will tell Ms. Williams when it's over."

"All right, Mr. Banner, you have my word."

"You know of the four murders that have taken place that had the phrase 'Eagle Down' attached to them," Clive started.

"Yes," Sam responded.

"Well, Dan here thought he would try to run down and find out what that phrase meant. He was working with your reporters. They found the file that the woman Patricia Manning had. Here it is. Read it before we go on any further."

Clive handed the file to Sam. He read it without saying a word, and when he finished reading, he looked up at Clive and said, "Is this for real?"

"I'm afraid so, Mr. Corcoran. Four people have died because of it."

"God Almighty! The president and the vice president. That would make Giddings president."

"That's right, and you'll notice, whoever is behind this plot doesn't want the stimulus bill to pass."

Sam the asked, "Who is the Ghost?"

"We don't know. Probably some hired assassin."

Then Sam turned to Carol. "Young lady, you have done one hell of a job." Then he asked Banner, "Mr. Banner, can she continue to work with your agent here?"

Banner turned to Dan. "How about it, Dan?"

"It's fine with me," replied Dan.

Then they got up and left.

* * *

When Banner got back to his office, he called Richard Grander, director of the CIA. "Dick, Clive here. I need to get some information from you."

"Sure, Clive. What do you need?"

"Have you ever heard of a professional assassin called the Ghost?"

He thought for a moment then replied, "No, can't say that I have. Is he foreign or domestic?"

"I don't think he's domestic."

"Okay, I'll search our files. If I can't find him there, I'll call Interpol. If he's in Europe or Asia, they will have him in their files. I'll call you back."

Half an hour later, Clive's phone rang. "Clive, I found your Ghost. He's a hired assassin who works in Europe and Asia. Interpol has him in their files."

"Can we get a photo of him and prints or DNA?"

"No. They have nothing on him, no photo or anything else. They know he exists. He is very elusive. That's why they call him the Ghost. They gave him credit for four known assassinations in Europe and one in Asia. Apparently, he only takes assassinations of high-profile leaders and is very expensive. He has no known MO. He has used explosives, long-range rifles, and car bombings. What interest do you have in this character, Clive?"

"Keep this under your hat, Dick, but we have evidence that the president and vice president have received a threat of assassination."

"By this Ghost?"

"Yes. What does Interpol have on this guy?"

"I don't know. I'll have Interpol call you."

"Fine, but I'm going to ask you to work with us on this one, Dick."

"Hold on, Clive. You know the CIA cannot operate in domestic affairs."

"Yes, I understand. But if this character is from Europe or Asia, then you can work on that angle."

"Yes, you're right. I'll call Interpol and see what I can get."

An hour later, Clive's secretary buzzed Clive on his intercom. "Yes?" he answered.

"Sir, an Inspector Byron Cunningham is on the line for you. He says he's from Interpol. Shall I put him through? He's on line 1."

"Yes, by all means." Clive picked up his phone. "Hello, Mr. Cunningham?"

"Yes. I got several calls from your CIA director, Richard Grander, about an assassin known as the Ghost. What is your interest in him? He has only operated in Europe and Asia so far."

"Well, Cunningham, I think he has expanded his territory."

"Has he threatened any of your people?"

"Yes."

"Who?"

"I'm afraid I'm not at a liberty to say."

"Come on, Mr. Banner. You are talking to a high person in Europe's best law enforcement organization. We can be trusted to keep your secret."

"I guess you're right. We have credible evidence of a plot to assassinate our president and vice president. And the assassin will be the Ghost."

"I say, Mr. Banner, you do have a sticky wicket there, don't you?"

"Yes, whatever that is."

"Mr. Banner, we have been after this Ghost character for several years. He has been very elusive. Would you object to me coming over to your shore and working with you to capture this man?"

"No, not at all. I would welcome your expertise," Clive said.

"Thank you. I'll catch a flight tomorrow and see you in your office the day after. Good day, sir."

"Good day to you, Inspector Cunningham."

Clive called Richard Grander. "Dick, I got a call from Cunningham of Interpol. He's coming to the States tomorrow and will be in my office the day after. I would like you to handle him. After all, he's foreign."

"Be glad to, Clive. I've worked with him before."

* * *

At the Cairo International Airport, a pilot was doing a final preflight check on a Cessna Citation X jet plane. It was a sleek plane with two jet engines and a ceiling of fifty thousand feet capable of traveling six hundred miles an hour. A black Cadillac limo drove up beside the plane, and a man got out of the limo, stretched his legs, and walked over to the pilot checking the jet. He was an Arab with short tightly curled black hair. His skin was dark, and he was wearing dark sunglasses. He was a tall man, just a little under six feet, and slim. He was dressed in a very expensive silk suit.

"Just about ready?" asked the Arab.

The pilot turned around and said, "Just about, sir. She's fully fueled, and I'm just about finished with the final outside preflight check."

"Good," said the Arab. "I'll be in the cockpit. When you are through, I'll give you our destination. Then you can file a flight plan."

"Very well, sir."

When the pilot had completed his outside preflight check, he came into the cockpit and sat down in the left seat. The Arab was a qualified pilot and certified to fly the Citation, but he preferred to relax and let the other man fly the plane.

"Our destination is Tehran Imam Khomeini International Airport in Tehran, Iran. Ask the tower for a flight level of 35. I want to fly high over Israel, Jordan, and Iraq."

"Yes, sir," said the pilot, and he proceeded to put all the flight data in the plane's computer. When he was through, he radioed the tower and gave them a flight plan. Then he and the Arab did a pre-flight check in the cockpit. When it was complete, they started the engines, got clearance to taxi to the runway, and waited for takeoff clearance. When the tower gave them clearance, they roared down the runway and into the sky.

When they landed in Tehran, the Arab said to the pilot, "Go to the hotel just outside the airport. We will be here several days, maybe a week. I have to get in touch with the mechanics to modify the plane. I'll call you when we are ready to leave."

After the pilot left, the Arab made a phone call. The answering party said, "Yes?"

The Arab said, "This is Abdul. Do you have the parts and the missile?"

"Yes! It's a fatter made in Iran, a copy of the United States' sidewinder, and I have the launcher for under the wing and the electronics."

"Good. How long will it take to modify the plane?"

"A week, maybe less."

"The plane is parked just to the left of your hangar." Then Abdul gave him the tail number of the plane. "Call me when you finish. I'll be in the airport hotel."

* * *

Timothy Hendricks came into the oval office. The president greeted him. "Hi, Tim. What's so urgent it couldn't wait? I had to cancel my meeting with an ambassador."

"Sir, read this document," Hendricks said as he handed the president the Eagle Down document.

The president read it while standing in front of his couch. When he finished, he had a glassy-eyed look on his face. Still staring, he sat down on the couch and turned to Hendricks. "Is this real?" he asked.

"Yes, sir. We believe it to be real. This is what your assistant chief of staff was killed for, to keep this under wraps."

"My god, kill the president and vice president to keep the stimulus bill from becoming law? This seems impossible," the president said. "Who is this Ghost?"

"We don't know. We suspect he's a hired assassin living in Europe or Asia. We have Interpol looking into it."

"Who is behind this?"

"At this juncture, we don't know."

"Giddings and Saxton could be the only ones to gain if the vice president and I were assassinated. They are dead set against my bill. I can't believe those honorable men could stoop to this level."

Tim said, "Well, remember, sir, we don't know who's behind this. This document was just discovered today. We are going to take extra precautions to protect you and the vice president. I might ask you to cut back on your travels."

"I can't do that, Tim. I have to be out there with the public, pushing my bill. Otherwise, it's lost. I'm going to call Grace Arden and have her come in here. She should know if someone is trying to kill her."

When Grace Arden, the vice president, came into the oval office, the president handed her the Eagle Down document. "Grace, read this."

As she read, she kept looking up at Harrison. When she finished, she looked down with the document in her lap then looked up at Harrison. "Is this a joke?"

"No, Grace. Timothy here and Clive Banner think this is a real threat. The service is going to beef up their guard on you and me. Until this madman is caught, be on your guard. I'd hate to lose the best member of our team. Be sure you do everything your agents tell you," the president said.

* * *

Clive was reading a report when his secretary buzzed him on the intercom. "Yes?" he said.

"Inspector Cunningham is here to see you."

"Oh, send him in."

When Cunningham came in, he looked like a typical English gentleman. He was wearing a fedora, had a bushy blond mustache, and was tall and thin. He walked across the room to Clive's desk, stuck out his hand, and said, "Jolly good to meet you, old man." He spoke with a distinct English accent.

Clive stood up, reached across his desk, and took the Englishman's hand. "How do you do, sir? Sit down."

The man sat down and waited for Clive to say something.

Finally, Clive asked, "How was your trip?"

"Oh, jolly good. Have you anything new on the Ghost fellow?"

"No, but here is what we have so far." He handed Cunningham the Eagle Down document.

Cunningham read it and said, "I say this is a bloody mess, killing two of your administration people. Do you know who cooked up this plot?"

"No, not yet. I'm mustering all our efforts to find this Ghost."

"This document mentions a stimulus bill. What's that about?"

"The country, as you know, is in a deep recession. Our president has proposed a very large spending bill to help the country regain its economy. It's very controversial. The debate is going on not only in our congressional bodies but also on every street corner in the United States."

"Yes, old man, we have the same economic problems in Great Britain."

"It appears some factions are dead set against the bill being passed and have taken this extraordinary measure to block the vote. The two people mentioned in that document will replace our president and vice president."

"Then they could be behind this plot, eh?"

"I suppose, but that's jumping to a conclusion. We have absolutely no proof that they even know about the plot."

"In Great Britain, we have a planned succession to the throne if our monarch dies. Do you have something similar here?"

"Yes. If the president dies, or resigns, like in the case of Richard Nixon, then the vice president becomes the president. If she dies, then the speaker of the house takes over."

"Are either one of the gentlemen in this document in line for the president?"

"Yes, the House speaker, Samuel Giddings."

Then the man from Interpol said, "Then, old man, I suggest that he is behind the plot."

"Could be. But again, it's a bit early to point fingers without any proof."

"Well, you best be the judge of that in your country."

"Inspector Cunningham, I'm going to call our CIA director to come over here and meet you. He works with problems dealing with covert operations outside the United States. Since this Ghost is from outside our territory, he will be leading the investigation outside our borders. I will head up the investigation in this country. Of course, the Secret Service has been informed of this plot and is taking precautionary measures to protect the president and vice president. One other aspect of this case is murder."

"I should hope so if they are going to kill your president."

"No, Inspector, I mean in addition to the plot, we have had four murders of people who were aware that this plot existed."

"Oh my. Are any more people in danger?"

"I don't think so. Now that we have the document, there won't be any attempts to hide it. But we are looking for the man who killed them."

"Do you know who he is?"

"No, but we have an artist's sketch of him, one before he disguised himself and one after."

"I say, if you could give me copies of this man, I could have my colleagues search our files in London. He may be from the Far East. We might get lucky."

Clive reached into his drawer and took out the two sketches. "Here you go, Inspector."

He handed the sketches to the inspector. "Do you have a fax in your office, Mr. Banner?"

"Yes."

"Could you have your secretary come in? I'll give her the phone number of my fax in London and instructions for my office to check out this bloke."

While Cunningham was dictating to Clive's secretary, Clive phoned Richard Grander. "Dick, Inspector Cunningham is in my office. Would you come get him?"

"Sure. Be right over," Richard said.

* * *

Later that afternoon, Clive got a call from Richard Grander. "Clive, I have good news for you."

"What's that, Dick?"

"Interpol has identified your killer."

"You mean the Ghost?"

"No. The man who murdered those four people. He's an Arab from Yemen. His name is Hassan Kahil. Interpol sent a photo of him to my office. I'll have a courier run it over to you. You can get it on the wire and in the newspapers. He's wanted in Great Britain, France, and Germany for murders in all three countries. He doesn't go in for high-profile leaders. His specialty is low-level politicians and executives of large companies. Interpol says he probably came into our country with a forged passport from Saudi Arabia."

"If we get his picture pasted all over, with a picture of him without hair on his face and head, we might get lucky."

"I think you might want to get with the airlines and airports with this picture. If this guy sees his picture all over, he's going to split."

"Yes, and we'll cover the bus companies as well. He might want to take a bus to Canada or Mexico to get out of the country. You might want to alert the Canadians and Mexican authorities, in case he slips through."

"Good point, Dick."

"Clive, I've been thinking. We should get together with Secret Service and make a plan. That way, we all know what's going on."

"What do you mean?"

"Well, for one thing, if the president is going to travel somewhere, we should know about it. That way, we can take extra precautions. I know the Secret Service will be on full alert, but if he goes to Cleveland, for instance, you can have your agents in Cleveland notified and be on full alert."

"I guess you're right, Dick. I'll call Timothy Hendricks."

* * *

Carol was at her desk when Dan called. "Hi, doll. Got something for you."

"Something I can print?"

"Yep. We found out who our killer is."

"You did?"

"Yes. He's an Arab named Hassan Kahil. He's from Yemen. He was identified by Interpol. He's wanted in three countries in Europe for assassination of politicians and executives of large companies. I'll fax you his picture and ask your paper to print it along with the artist's sketch of him without hair. I'll also send the purported murders he is suspected of committing. It should make a good story for your paper. You realize you are getting an exclusive on this."

"Yes, Dan, and thanks."

Carol hurried down to Sam's office. She rushed into his office. Her face was flushed with excitement. "Hold the presses," she said with a smile.

Sam looked up. "Are you kidding? Do you have something?"

"Yes, Chief, a big story!"

"Well, let's have it."

"The CIA went to Interpol with the sketch of our killer. You know, the one who killed the Bigelows and the others."

"And?"

"They identified him. His name is Hassan Kahil. He's from Yemen and wanted by Interpol, Britain, France, and Germany."

"Where did you get this information? Are you sure it's verified?"

"Yes. I got a call from Dan Morris, right from the horse's mouth: the FBI. He asked us to print it."

Sam picked up his phone and dialed. When someone picked up the phone on the other end, he said, "Pressroom? Hold up on print. I have another front-page story." He hung up and said to Carol, "Okay, gal, go write it, and pronto. I'll hold up the presses."

* * *

The paper hit the streets with this headline: killer identified.

Hassan was in his room, watching TV, when his cell phone rang. "Yes?" he answered.

"Have you read the paper today?" the voice asked.

"No. I haven't been out of my room. What's in the paper?"

"You've been identified. Your picture is all over the front page. Your picture from Interpol and the FBI artist sketch without your hair."

"How did that happen? I kept undercover."

"I don't know, but you'll have to get out of the country. The paper says they are starting a manhunt for you. Local cops and the FBI."

"I'd better stay away from the airports. That's the first place they'll look."

"Can you stay in your room until it cools down?"

"Yes. For a few days. But then I have to go out and get some food."

"Well, be careful. They are going to cover this area like a blanket."

"What about my money?"

"It's been deposited in your Swiss bank account."

"How will I know when the heat is off?"

"I'll keep tabs with the FBI and let you know."

* * *

A week had passed since landing in Tehran when Abdul received a phone call from the mechanic who altered his jet. "Abdul, the plane is ready."

"Is the missile in the cargo hold?"

"Yes, and lashed down. Tell your pilot I will show him how to mount the missile and how to arm it and fire it. It is an infrared missile, heat-seeking, so you will need to get close to launch it."

"Will it take down a Boeing 747?"

"Without a doubt. It has enough explosive power to blow off the tail and then some. It was designed to completely blow up a small fighter. It will seek out the jet engines, and if you hit it, it will disintegrate the wing and engine and spray debris all over the aircraft. Have no fear, brother. This will do the job."

* * *

The next morning, Abdul, the pilot, and the mechanic were at the hangar. The mechanic showed the two men how to place and hook up the missile to a hard point on the wing. Then, inside the cockpit, he showed them how to arm the missile and finally how to launch it.

When they were ready to leave, the pilot gave the tower a flight plan. First stop for refueling was Trondelag, Sweden, then Iceland and Winnipeg, Canada. Abdul's plan was to get into the United States undetected. When they left Winnipeg, they filed no flight plan; they were flying VFR (visual flight rules) at ten thousand feet. Before they reached the border, Abdul took the plane down to five hundred feet near an airport that had no tower. To air traffic control, it appeared that the plane landed at the airport and left their screen. Then, when the terrain was available, he dropped the plane down to treetop level and reduced his air speed, crossing the border into the United States. The Citation X jet was not on the radar screen. He flew at this level for several hundred miles. Then near an airport without a tower, he took the plane back up to several thousand feet. He was picked up on radar from air traffic control and appeared to be a plane taking off from an airport flying VFR squawking 1,200 on his transponder. They flew at five thousand feet to Billings, Montana, and landed.

Abdul, the Ghost, was now in the United States undetected. He had a forged driver's license from the state of Montana, which was all he needed to fly in commercial jets in the United States.

CHAPTER 6

The manhunt for Hassan Kahil was enormous. Every available FBI agent, every Washington, DC, officer, and every sheriff's department deputy was in on the search. Every checkpoint at every airport within one hundred miles of Washington had Hassan's picture posted. Every hotel and restaurant in the same area had his picture. All car body repair shops were visited by the FBI to see if Hassan had taken his car in to repair the damage to the body of the Mercedes when he pushed Bob and Carol off the road. All police cruisers were on the lookout for a black Mercedes with damage to the right side of the body and fenders. Hassan was the only link to the perpetrators of the plot. The FBI hoped that if they found Hassan, he might lead them to the Ghost and foil the plot before it started. They had no idea how or when the Ghost would make an attempt to assassinate the president and vice president.

Clive Banner sat in the office of Timothy Hendricks, the head of the Secret Service. "Tim, I talked to Inspector Cunningham of Interpol about the various methods the Ghost has used to assassinate his victims. Apparently, he has no favorite method. One time, he used a high-powered rifle. Another time, he used an RPG rocket. One time, he used a bomb under the vehicle. Interpol thinks he changes his method depending on the security the victim has and the traveling method the victim uses. Can you protect the president from any and all methods?"

"I believe we can, Clive. The limo the president travels in is bulletproof and can withstand a blast from explosives—a reasonable amount, that is. I doubt that he can get past our security guards in the White House. We have men on the roof of the White House and have antiaircraft guns there also in case a plane breaks through the restricted, no-fly zone."

"Is Air Force One vulnerable in the air?"

"Air Force One is equipped with missile detectors, and it has countermeasures that can be released to fool the missile. I suppose, if a pilot would be willing to give up his life, he could crash into the 747 in flight. But it would have to be a fast jet to catch the Boeing 747. If any foreign fighter jets tried to enter the country, they would be detected by NORAD, and fighters would be sent up to intercept them, so I think we are safe there. I have tried to get the president to cut down on his traveling speaking engagements, but he feels he must get out with the public and push his stimulus plan."

"Why take the risk?"

"The president feels like he needs the public behind him to force a vote on the stimulus bill. If the bill passes, that will negate the plot."

"I doubt it. If the bill passes and the president is assassinated, then the new president and vice president will simply have a new bill, eliminating the first one. The only way we have to protect the president is to find this Ghost fellow and the people behind this plot."

"I'll pass your comments on to the president, Clive."

* * *

Abdul and his pilot rented a car and checked into a motel. Abdul told his pilot he was going to Washington to meet with Hassan Kahil. "I need to find out the president's schedule." He bought an airline ticket from Billings, Montana, to Washington, DC, landing at Reagan International Airport. He boarded the *Eagle Down* flight and took his first-class seat. The flight took three and a half hours. When the flight landed, he had no luggage, so he went directly to the outside of the terminal, where he hailed a cab. He gave the cabbie the address of Hassan Kahil. When he knocked on the door, Hassan did not open it. Instead, he asked, "Who's there?" through the door.

Abdul replied, "It's Abdul."

Hassan smiled and opened the door. The two men embraced, and Abdul said, "What's going on, Hassan? I saw your picture in the airport terminal." He looked at Hassan and asked, "Why did you shave off your hair?"

"The FBI has identified me as the killer of some people that I eliminated to keep this plan from being discovered."

"It's still a secret, is it not?"

"Yes. The authorities have not found out about it yet. They know the name of this project but have no idea what it's about."

"Good. If they knew, it would make my job a little more difficult. I doubt if they would ever guess how I plan on taking out those two people."

"Why are you here, Abdul?"

"I need to get the president's itinerary. It would be most helpful if I got his schedule, especially when he and the vice president travel together."

"I will call my contact and see if I can get it for you."

"When are you planning to execute your plan?"

"That depends on when the president's travel puts him close to the Canadian border."

"Why the Canadian border?"

"After I take out Air Force One, every fighter in this country will be in the air, looking for me. I need to get across the border and land until the heat is off then fly back to Cairo. So I want to be as close to the border as possible. I've read that the president is making cross-country trips to sell his bill. When he comes close to the border, that's when I will strike."

"How are you planning on taking this Air Force One out?"

"That, my friend, will remain a secret until I do it."

"I will phone my contact now."

Hassan used his cell phone to call his contact. On the other line, a voice said, "I know who you are. I cannot talk now. I will call you back in half an hour."

The two men sat around and talked about the Middle East, where they both were from, until Hassan's phone rang. He opened it and said, "Yes?"

"I'm sorry. I was in a meeting and couldn't talk with all those people in the room. What can I do for you?"

"I have your man here in my apartment."

"The Ghost?"

"Yes, and he needs something."

"What? If I can get it, I will."

"He would like the president's schedule for his trips in Air Force One."

"Air Force One?"

"Yes."

"What does he need that for? It's very hard to come by."

"Just a moment."

Hassan held his hand over the mouthpiece of his phone, looked at Abdul, and said, "He wants to know why you need that information."

"Tell him I do not give information of my plans to anyone. That is why I have been so successful. But I need that information. Tell him!"

"He says that he cannot tell you why he needs that information, but he needs it."

"Ask him when he will complete his mission."

Again, Hassan asked Abdul, "He wants to know when you will strike."

"Tell him it was our agreement that I would not tell him where or when I will strike. The less the client knows, the more success I will have."

Hassan repeated what Abdul said.

"Okay. When does he need this information?" the voice asked.

Hassan asked Abdul, "He wants to know when you need this information."

"Tell him right away."

"He says right away," Hassan said.

"Okay, I'll see what I can do. Will he be with you until I get this information?"

"Yes!"

***

George Saxton called Sam Giddings. "I need to see you right away. Can you come to my office?"

"Sure, George. Be right there."

When Samuel came into George's office and sat down, he asked, "You sounded urgent. What's up?"

"I got a call from our contact for Eagle Down."

"Is he still hiding?"

"Yes, and he has the Ghost there with him."

"He's in the States?"

"Yes, and he needs some information."

"What kind of information?"

"The president's plane schedule."

"What would he need that for? Wait a minute. Do you think he will take Air Force One down as it leaves the ground?"

"Could be. I really don't know."

"George, that airport is surrounded with all military personnel. He couldn't get close enough to fire a handheld missile."

"Sam, I don't know what his plans are. All he wants is the president's schedule."

"Can you get it?"

"I have some contacts in the White House. I'll try them first."

"And if that doesn't work?"

"I have another plan. I'll ask the president directly."

"Damn, George, won't that tip him off?"

"Naw. Why should it? I'll just tell him I might want to go with him on one of his trips to see how the public is buying his bill. He won't suspect anything. Look, I don't have any idea why the Ghost wants that information. But I'll tell you, Sam, I won't set foot on Air Force One, not knowing what the Ghost is up to."

"Well, no one knows about our plan, so he would have no reason to suspect why you want his schedule."

***

Gerald Harrison's secretary buzzed him on his intercom and said, "Mr. President, Senator Saxton called and said he would like to come to the White House and talk to you."

"Did he say why he wanted to see me?"

"No, sir. Just said he wanted to see you."

"Okay. Do I have any time open today?" the president asked.

"Yes, sir, between three and three thirty."

"Okay, schedule him then and ask Paul Barrows to join us."

At three o'clock, Senator Saxton walked into the oval office. Paul Barrows was already there, and he and the president were sitting on the couch. "Good afternoon, Mr. President, and you, Paul."

"Good afternoon, George. Why did you want to see me? Is it about my bill?"

"Well, yes and no."

"Let's hear it, George. I'm getting frustrated at how slow my bill is moving through Congress."

"Well, as you know, it takes sixty votes in the Senate to pass a bill. Your party doesn't have that majority, so it's going to take a hard sell to convince my party members to come around to your thinking, if they do at all."

"When can your committee bring the bill up for a vote?"

George said, "Can't say. No use in voting if the preliminary count will defeat it."

"All right, George. What's on your mind?"

"I was wondering if you would consider taking me along on one of your stomping trips to sell your bill."

"Why, George? You are opposed to my bill."

"Don't misunderstand. I would not get up and openly oppose you. I would like to get a feel for how the people feel about your plan. You know, if the polls show you are gaining ground, I could swing some votes in the Senate your way."

"All right, George. That sounds reasonable. When would you like to go?"

"I can't say. I have many engagements in the Senate. Perhaps it would be best if you gave me your schedule and I could try to fit a trip in my schedule."

"Okay. Paul, give George a copy of my travel schedule for the next month. But, George, keep it to yourself. The Secret Service would be unhappy if they knew someone had an advanced copy of my travel schedule. The vice president goes with me on these trips. She's very popular and draws a big crowd."

"Yes. You were smart to have Grace Arden, a woman, on your ticket. I think that helped swing the election for you. Of course, Mr. President, your schedule will be safe with me. And, Paul, I'll let you know when I can fit my schedule into the president's."

When Saxton got back to his office, he phoned Hassan. "Tell the Ghost I have the president's planned flight schedule for the next month. I will e-mail it to you and send the schedule as an attachment. Did he say why he needs this schedule?"

"No. Only that he needed it."

"Sounds to me like he is trying to blow up Air Force One."

"I do not know. He does not speak about his plans."

When Abdul received the president's schedule, he noticed there was an asterisk beside most of the scheduled trips. On the bottom of the schedule was an asterisk, and alongside it, it said, "Vice president attending."

He smiled. This made his job much easier. Now he could get both of them at the same time.

As he was leaving, Abdul said to Hassan, "My friend, you were a big help. If you have any jobs in Europe or Asia and need help, call on me."

Then he left and flew back to Billings, Montana. When he arrived, he arranged to rent a private hangar for his Citation jet. He and his pilot would place the missile on the wing of the jet. He wanted no one to see the missile. It would be a dead giveaway that something was amiss and bring authorities to question the need for a private jet with an air-to-air missile. Armament of that kind was not allowed on a public airport. Missiles were only present on military jets stationed on military airfields.

* * *

Clive Banner called a meeting with Dan Morris, several of his staff, and Timothy Hendricks of the Secret Service. When they were all seated, he stood up. "Gentlemen, I called this meeting to find out where we are in finding Hassan Kahil and how close we are to rooting out the perpetrators of this plot. Dan, you go first."

"Well, sir, we have every airport terminal, railroad station, and bus depot covered. We have talked to every body shop within a hundred miles of Washington. The local police are on the lookout for a black Mercedes with damage to the right side. And so far, we have no hints or clues where this guy is. I suspect when he saw his picture and name in the paper, he holed up and decided not to go on the street for fear of being recognized. There is nothing else we can do. I plan on having the *Washington Ledger* keep the story on the front page, as well as his picture. That way, if he comes out of hiding, hopefully someone will recognize him and call us."

"Clive, there is more than one leg on this stool," said Timothy. "As I see it, we have Hassan, the Ghost, and whoever is behind this plot. What are we doing in these other areas?"

"The CIA is working with Interpol to see if they can find the Ghost or find out if he's even in this country. Frankly, I don't have much hope there. They don't know what this guy looks like or any names he might have used as aliases. They don't know what his nationality is. They have nothing. The intelligence at Interpol says he has used numerous methods to take out his victims."

"Well, what about the men behind the plot?"

"Again, we have nothing."

Tim said, "I don't know about that. You have Harry Bigelow sending an e-mail to George Saxton and Admiral Goodman asking about Eagle Down. In addition, Saxton will gain from the deaths of the president and vice president, as well as Sam Giddings."

"But, Tim, that's only circumstantial."

"But that's all you've got. Shouldn't you follow up on that?"

"How?"

"Put a tap on their phones in their offices and homes. Both men have cell phones. Listen in on their conversations."

"I would need a federal judge to give me a warrant to bug them," Clive said.

"Go to the attorney general and ask him to get it for you. Christ, you have done it numerous times."

"Yes, for criminals, not the two highest positions in our government: the leaders of the House and Senate."

"Clive, they are men—just men—and subject to human temptations. They would gain power and prestige if the president and vice president would die."

"Okay, I'll get the warrant."

* * *

George Saxton was a married man and had a son in college, so only Saxton and his wife occupied the home. When Saxton left for the Senate building in the morning, a team of technicians was waiting for his wife to leave home. They sat in a van not far from Saxton's house. The van had the name of the local telephone company painted on its side. They knew his wife was a social butterfly and belonged to many social organizations. After waiting two days, Isabel, George's wife, left the house to go to one of her social functions. As soon as she did, the van pulled up in the driveway. Five men got out of the van, dressed in overalls, with the name of the telephone company emblazoned on the back of the overalls in case neighbors were watching. They carried a lot of equipment into the house.

They put bugs in the mouthpieces of all the telephones, under the kitchen and dining room tables, under tables in the living room, and in George's study, any place that Saxton might have a conversation with a conspirator. They put a small camera in the ceiling fan in his study and a recorder in his attic to capture the picture and sound. They were through in an hour and left long before Isabel returned.

Then a black van with two men in it parked up the street to listen in on the phone calls and any conversation in the house. Then they went to Samuel Giddings house and planted the same bugs and camera.

When the offices of the Senate and House of Representative adjourned for the night, the FBI came in and bugged the office of Sam Giddings and George Saxton. Now they had both men in a position that if they talked to anyone about the plot on any of the phones, they would be overheard and recorded. So now they just sat and waited.

* * *

Bob Grant was out of the hospital. His concussion was cured. He walked into the newspaper office one morning and sat down at his desk. Carol looked up and was surprised to see him. "Hey, Bob, I didn't expect to see you so soon. Did the doctors say you could return to work?"

"Yeah, but no strenuous work of any kind for a month. I tried just sitting around watching TV, but that drove me crazy, watching all those crappy daytime shows. I would rather be here, working. What's new on the Eagle Down story?"

"We found the folder that Patricia Manning had in her safe-deposit box. Damn, Bob, that file is incredible."

Excited, Bob asked, "What was in it?"

"Sam and I have been sworn to secrecy, but I guess since we're both working on the same story, you should know. But if I tell you what the contents are, you can't discuss it with anyone but Sam, me, or the FBI. Agreed?"

"Yes. Now, what the hell is so secret about Eagle Down?"

"It's a plot to kill the president and vice president and kill the stimulus bill. The perpetrators have hired an assassin named the Ghost. No one in this country has heard of him before, but Interpol is aware that he exists. They have been trying to locate him for years. Interpol says he's been behind a number of assassinations in Europe and Asia. The FBI and Secret Service are working together to try to locate him and the killer of the Bigelows, Patricia Manning, and Jerry Baldwin. We now know his name. It's Hassan Kahil. He was in Interpol files, and his picture is posted all over the area."

"So how is this Ghost fellow going to kill the president and VP?"

"We don't know. Secret Service is beefing up the protection of them both. But we are getting an exclusive on this story. I'm working with Dan Morris. The FBI director, Clive Banning, gave his approval to have Dan and me work together. They want the paper to keep putting the story on the front page and maybe drive this Hassan fellow out in the open," Carol said.

* * *

Clive Banner and Timothy Hendricks went to see the president to discuss the assassination plot. When they were seated, Gerald Harrison asked, "What about this fellow the Ghost? Do you have anything new on him?"

"No, Mr. President," replied Clive. "Interpol is working with the CIA to see if they can identify him. He's a citizen of one of the countries in the Far East, as far as they can tell. Which country, they don't know."

"So if you have nothing new on him, what did you want to talk about?"

"Dick here and I were talking about who is behind this plot. It seems to us that Giddings and Saxton have the most to gain if you and the vice president were assassinated. Not only would they get the two top posts in the country, they would also be able to kill your stimulus bill. I doubt that if it were someone else, they would have talked to those gentlemen. You just don't say I will make George Saxton vice president. You have to have some authority to do that, like Samuel Giddings, when he would become president."

"Then you consider those two men your prime candidates as the perpetrators."

"Yes. Now, what I'm proposing is to tell George and Sam that we have uncovered the plot. We know about Eagle Down."

"Won't that just make them more cautious?"

"Yes, but it will force their hand if I tell them we consider them the prime suspects behind the plot."

"What do you expect to gain from that?"

"One of two things: they may call off their plot or get in contact with the Ghost. We have all their lines tapped. If either one of them tries to contact the Ghost, it may just lead us to him. If the Ghost is going to attempt the assassination, he will undoubtedly do it before the bill comes up for a vote. My guess is that he's in this country right now, just waiting to take you down."

"But you can't accuse a man without any proof, Clive."

"I'm not going to accuse him. I'm going to point out that he and Giddings have the most to gain and that we will be watching them."

When he got back to his office, Clive phoned Saxton. "Hello, George. I wonder if I could prevail on you to come to my office."

"Sure, Clive. What's it about?"

"A project known as Eagle Down."

"Eagle Down? You asked me about that before, Clive, and I told you I knew nothing about that."

"I know. But something new has come up, and I think you should be apprised of it."

"Okay, if you think it's important."

"I do. How about three this afternoon?"

"Fine, I'll be there."

Then he phoned Sam Giddings, and he agreed to meet with Clive.

At ten minutes to three, Sam came into Clive's office. "Sit down, Sam. I have another person in this meeting. He should be here soon."

At three o'clock sharp, George Saxton came in. When he saw Sam Giddings, he stopped short. "Hello, Sam. What are you doing here?"

"I was invited by Clive. I don't know what this is about."

Clive spoke up. "Sit down, Senator, and I'll get to the meat of this meeting."

Saxton sat down with a quizzical look on his face. "Okay, Clive. Shoot."

"Gentlemen, we have uncovered a plot to kill the president and the vice president by an assassin known as the Ghost and then kill the stimulus bill."

"What?" said Saxton. Giddings's face turned white. Clive waited for them to say something. Then Saxton laughed and said, "You must be joking. That's preposterous. Who would want to kill the president? Some nut?"

"No, George. Someone who has a lot to gain."

"And who would that be?" asked Giddings.

"For one, you, Sam. If the president and vice president are assassinated, you are in line for the presidency. Am I not correct?"

"Yes, that's true. Are you suggesting I am behind this plot?"

"No, but you have the most to gain: power and prestige. And in this plot, George, you will be made vice president by Sam here nominating you. Then your party will have enough power to kill the stimulus bill, which they are dead set against."

"It sounds to me, Clive," said Giddings, "that you are accusing us of being behind this plot. Do you have anything—anything at all—to back up your accusations?"

"Gentlemen, I am not—and I repeat, am not—accusing either of you of being behind this plot. I am merely pointing out that you two have the most to gain from an assassination of our president and vice president and that we, the FBI, will be watching both of you."

"You mean keep us both under surveillance?"

"Perhaps, but not that you would notice."

Saxton stood up. "Clive, you have practically accused us of attempting to murder two people, two of the most powerful people in this country. That infuriates me. I don't know about you, Sam, but I'm leaving. Clive, if I hear one word about this plot and I am implicated, I'll sue you. You can be sure of that." Then he turned and left, with Sam Giddings right behind him.

Clive sat there with a broad smile on his face. In his mind, Saxton and Giddings were behind the plot. Now he had let the cat out of the bag. *So let's see where it goes,* he thought.

* * *

When the two men got outside the office building, Saxton said to Giddings, "Let's go to my office. We have to talk."

When they were in Saxton's office, Giddings sat down, but Saxton was pacing the floor. "I don't like it, Sam. Clive practically accused us of being behind the plot. I don't know where he got his information, but he was right on. I think he's getting close. We have to do something to throw him off track."

"What do you mean *do something*?"

George said, "Sam, he's got his whole damn cadre of agents looking for Hassan and the Ghost. We need a diversion."

"A diversion? What would take him off the track?"

"Something big."

"Like what?"

I don't know. Maybe something like the bombing of the Alfred P. Murrah Building in Oklahoma City."

"You mean Timothy McVeigh? The guy that was executed?"

"Yeah, but nothing that big. I know. How about a bomb in the FBI building garage?"

"Blow up the FBI building! No, George, that's out. I can't, in good conscience, kill a big group of people!"

"No, I don't mean blow up the whole building, just a bomb in the underground garage. That will get their attention and pull some of their agents off us and Hassan and give the Ghost time to act. I'm sure having their building hit with a bomb will really make them mad that someone could get at them, the best law enforcement agency in the nation."

"Do you think Hassan can do it? After all, every cop for fifty miles around is looking for him," Sam asked.

"Yes. He's evaded the police in Europe for over ten years. He always has three or four disguises ready to go. Sam, we have to do something to get Clive off our backs. If he keeps digging, he may come up with something. Remember, he found out about the plan. Where he got his information is beyond me. But he got it."

"Okay, George, but make it a small bomb. I don't want people killed."

***

Later, Saxton used his cell phone and called Hassan. "Hello. You know who this is."

"Yes!"

"We need to meet."

"Okay."

"The same place tonight at eight o'clock."

"I'll be there."

***

Later that night, at seven thirty, Hassan went to a briefcase and opened it. In it, he had several passports and driver's licenses to match and false beards and wigs as well as credit cards to match. He put on a blond wig and a false blond beard. He called a cab and left. When he got to a park bench where he and Saxton had met before, Saxton was already there. At first, Saxton didn't recognize him. When Hassan walked up to him, Saxton grinned. "I didn't recognize you at first."

"Good. What's on your mind? If it's about the Ghost, I have no knowledge of his whereabouts or when he will strike."

"No, it's not that. The FBI director knows about Eagle Down. Where he got his information, I don't know, and he suspects me as being behind the plot. I need something to distract him and get him off my trail."

"What did you have in mind?"

"Can you get into the FBI building parking garage?"

"I suppose I can," Hassan said.

"Can you make a small bomb and set it off in the garage?"

"Yes! What kind of damage do you want? Bring down the whole building?"

Saxton said, clarifying, "No. Just enough to take out the vehicles in the garage and maybe some damage to the first floor. Can you do that?"

"Yes. But it will cost you two hundred thousand."

"Damn! That's pretty steep."

"Look, I lose a van, and I have to go far and wide to get ammonium nitrate and nitromethane—that's a volatile racing fuel—and build a detonator. Then, of course, there's the risk, going into the lion's den when the lion is looking for me."

"Okay, I'll wire the money to your Swiss bank account first thing in the morning. When can you do the job?" Saxton asked.

"It will take me several days to gather up the material. Say, four days."

"Fine. Call me just before you go to the building to detonate the bomb."

* * *

The next morning, Hassan put on his blond wig and beard and sunglasses and called a cab. He took out the passport and driver's license that had his picture with the blond wig and beard and a credit card to match the name Peter Harmon. When the cab arrived, he told the driver, "Take me to the Reagan International Airport. I want to rent a car from the Handy Car Rental Agency."

At the airport, the cab let him off at the car rental company. He went in. The clerk at the desk asked, "Can I help you, sir?"

"Yes. I want to rent a van."

"Yes, sir. We have several."

"I want the one that can carry the most load."

"Okay. Can I have your driver's license and credit card?"

Hassan handed him the false license and his credit card. The clerk looked at his picture on the license then looked at Hassan. "Okay, Mr. Harmon, let me just put the data in the computer. It will be just a few minutes." When the clerk came back, he asked, "Do you want insurance, Mr. Harmon?"

"Yeah. Why not? I could get into an accident and total the whole damn thing."

"Yes, that could happen, God forbid. Here's your license back. Interesting, Mr. Harmon, you have an American name, but your skin is dark, like an Arabian. No offense. I mean, it's just unusual."

"That's because my father married an Arabian woman."

"I see. Now, just sign here, and I'll have someone bring the van up to the door."

As Hassan waited, a man drove the van up to the door, just as the clerk promised. It was a yellow Dodge van. He got in and drove off. The first place he went to was a paint shop he had called earlier. He pulled in and went into the office. A woman behind the counter asked, "Can I help you, sir?"

"Yes. I called earlier and asked if you could paint a name on both sides of my van. You said you could do it today. I made an appointment."

"Your name?"

"Harmon, Peter Harmon."

The woman looked into a book and said, "Yes, Mr. Harmon, we have you down. What did you want on your van?"

"Jiffy Plumbing. I want that on both sides."

She looked out the glass window separating the office from the shop. "I see your van is yellow. What color did you want the name?"

"Black."

"Any size letters?"

"No. Just so they stand out."

"Of course. Now, be seated, and I'll get our painter on your van right away."

Hassan waited in the lounge for an hour and a half. When the painter finished, Hassan was satisfied that the paint job looked professional, so he paid his bill and left. He went to his apartment, parking the van outside. He went through the yellow pages, looking for places to shop. Now he planned on going to a number of agriculture stores and buying small amounts of ammonium nitrate. He didn't want to raise any suspicions by buying a large quantity at any one location. Then he went to a racetrack in Virginia and bought a fifty-five-gallon drum of nitromethane, a highly volatile fuel used in racing cars. Finally, he went to an electronics store and bought parts to make an electronic detonator then returned home.

He spent the next few days building the detonator. When he tested it and was satisfied it worked, he was ready. Now all he needed were plumbers' tools to place in the back of the van in case the guard at the FBI garage checked it. He went to the local handyman store and bought plywood and a variety of plumbers' tools. In his garage, he cut the plywood so it would fit inside the van and shield the ammonium nitrate from view and used hooks on the plywood to hang tools. Now anyone looking into the back of the van would see the tools and not the ammonium nitrate and the fuel. He was now ready.

* * *

The next morning, he called Saxton. Saxton answered his cell phone. "Yes?"

"I'm ready. Today, this morning, is the time."

"Okay, but remember, kill no one."

"I will try, but I can't guarantee that."

Then they hung up. The agent listening to the call was puzzled. He heard the comment that the caller was ready then Saxton saying not to kill anyone. He went to his supervisor and played back the phone conversation on his recorder. "Tim, it sounds to me like they are planning something," he said to his supervisor.

"Yeah, but what? I'll take it up to Mr. Banner. Maybe he can make some sense out of it."

Banner sat and listened to the short conversation on the recorder then sat and thought for a minute. "That's it? Nothing more?" he asked.

"No, sir. But it sounds like something is going to happen today, this morning."

"Yes. But what? Where? We can't cover the whole city. I'll notify Timothy Hendricks in case it's a plot against the president or vice president."

* * *

Hassan's last touch was to type up a fake e-mail from the FBI office manager asking Jiffy Plumbing to come to the FBI headquarters and fix clogged plumbing in the restrooms. Then he put on his blond wig and beard and dressed in gray coveralls that plumbers wear, got in the van, and drove to the FBI building in the city. The FBI headquarters building was on Pennsylvania Avenue, between Ninth and Tenth Streets. It was a large building some seven stories tall. When Hassan drove in, he was stopped by a guard.

"What is your business here?" the guard asked. Hassan showed him the e-mail. The guard read it, went to the back of the van, looked through the rear-door window, and saw plumbing tools. Satisfied, he gave Hassan back the e-mail and raised the barrier for the van to pass through. Hassan parked temporarily in the middle of the garage. He went up on the elevator from the garage level to the first floor and walked around until he located the restrooms. In his mind, he estimated where the restrooms were on the floor plan of the building. He returned to the van and parked where he thought he was directly under the restrooms. This way, when the explosion went off, it would destroy the restrooms but not injure any people. He then set the timer on the detonator and went back up the elevator to the first floor and out the front door.

He walked a block and waited for the explosion. In fifteen minutes, the ammonium nitrate exploded with a tremendous roar heard for miles around the city of Washington. Hassan felt the concussion of the blast, and it almost knocked him down even though he was a block away. He watched and saw huge plumes of white smoke come out of the entrance to the garage. The guard shack, the barrier, and the guard were blown into the street. The whole building shook as the concussion went through the building, knocking many people who were standing down, sending furniture across the rooms, knocking over lamps and file cabinets, and breaking many windows. Everyone was terrified, and after the initial shock, people began to run for the exits. Several people got trampled in the rush to get to the doors. The building maintained its integrity, and other than a few cracks, a few small fires started in the garage and on the first floor. Most of the vehicles in the garage were either destroyed or severely damaged. The van disintegrated into a thousand pieces. The bomb left a huge hole on the first floor, the restrooms were gone, and part of the second floor was severely damaged.

Clive was in his office on the top floor, dictating to his secretary, when the explosion occurred. When the bomb went off, his chair and desk raised off the floor a few inches, all his pictures went to a crazy angle on the walls, his coatrack toppled over, and items on his desk fell. Clive's eyes widened, as did his secretary's. She screamed as she was knocked out of her chair. He momentarily waited before standing up, expecting something else to happen. He stood up and exclaimed, "Good God Almighty! What the hell was that?"

He went to his window and looked out. The street was filled with white smoke that came from the garage, and he saw people in the street running away from the building. Then he ran out of his office and saw employees running for the stairwells. He went back into his office, helped his secretary to her feet, and said, "Let's get out of here! There's been an explosion in the building."

The 911 operator was overwhelmed with calls. Soon, the streets were filled with police cruisers, fire engines, and ambulances. All employees in the building who were not hurt were standing around outside across the street, talking and looking at fires and smoke in the garage and first floor. When they arrived, firemen went into the first floor and found several dozen men and women on the floor, unconscious. They were taken out on stretchers and transported to the hospital. Some who could walk were assisted and sat down outside, trying to clear their heads.

George Saxton was in his office when he heard the explosion. He smiled. He knew Hassan had set off his bomb. Soon, he heard all the sirens racing through the city to the conflagration. Most employees in his office were calling friends to find out what had happened.

Hassan was satisfied that his bomb was a success. He walked a few blocks then hailed a cab to take him home. At home, he sat watching TV about all the news broadcasts concerning the bombing. He was very pleased with himself.

CHAPTER 7

When all the injured employees were taken to the hospital and the fires were put out, the fire department technicians and FBI forensics team searched the garage area of the FBI building to determine the cause of the blast.

Sam Corcoran was in his office, watching the news, when the broadcast was interrupted by a news bulletin. He called Carol and Bob into his office to watch the television broadcast. The broadcast said the Federal Bureau of Investigation building had been bombed. Forty people had been taken to the hospital, some in critical condition. So far, not all the people had been accounted for. It appeared the explosion had been in the underground garage. The broadcast claimed it was an act of terrorism by some unknown group.

Sam finally looked at Carol. "I felt that blast a while ago. I thought it was a sonic boom from one of our fighter aircraft. Who in the hell would want to bomb the FBI building?"

"Chief," Carol responded, "there are a lot of Islamic dissidents out there who would just be delighted to take out the FBI. The FBI has come down hard on them, trying to seek out and find these Islamic cells. Look at the building on the screen. They apparently didn't bring the building down. It's still standing, and none of the outside structure is harmed. It's not like the Oklahoma City bombing, when the Alfred P. Murrah Building was completely destroyed."

"Okay, you two get over there and see what you can find out. I know it's not your beat, but my other reporters are out on another assignment."

* * *

When they arrived near the FBI building, the streets were blocked off so no one could get near the building. The police let them pass the barricades when they showed their press passes. The street in front of the building was filled with fire engines and police cars with all their red, blue, yellow, and white lights flashing. As they worked their way closer to the underground garage, Bob saw a TV camera crew from one of the local stations. He asked the newsman, "Hi, Harry. Got anything for me?"

"No, Bob. Nothing except what I put out in my broadcast."

"What was that?"

"Someone or a group set off a bomb in the garage of the building. It did extensive damage to the garage and put a hole in the first floor. At last count, forty-one people have been taken to the hospital. So far, the firemen have found no one dead. I understand all the cars in the garage are pretty badly damaged. The rest of the building is untouched, except for minor damage, like broken windows. I saw Clive Banner come out a while back. I tried to get him on camera, but he refused and said he knew nothing and to wait until his forensic team completes their work."

"Has anyone claimed responsibility yet for the bombing?"

"Not that I've heard. But it's still a little early."

Bob and Carol brought along a cameraman. He took several pictures of the building. They waited around for another hour, but nothing new was discovered, so they went back to the paper to write the story.

Carol called Dan. "Do you know who bombed your building?"

"No. We suspect it was a terrorist group. Why, we don't know. Maybe because we are coming down hard on them."

She asked, "Could it be connected to Eagle Down?"

"I don't see how. No one knows that we know about the plot."

* * *

George Saxton was sitting in his office, watching the story on TV, when Sam Giddings came in. "Well, George, your man did a fair job. The building is still standing, and no one was killed."

"Yes. Now that ought to keep Clive and his boys busy for a while. This has got to be very embarrassing for him, the premier law enforcement organization in the country having their building bombed. That will show lack of security. I'll bet they put a lot of agents on this to find out who did this to them. That should take the heat off us for a while."

"Anything from the Ghost?"

"No. He told Hassan, when he does the job, then and only then will we know it's done and how."

"George, I can't hold the house indefinitely without a vote. The Ghost has got to act soon."

"Well, the president's schedule I gave him only goes for thirty days, so I assume he will act within that timetable."

"I hope so. I was thinking last night. Where did Clive get the story on Eagle Down?"

"My guess is from the woman in my office."

"You mean that Patricia woman that Hassan killed?"

"Yes. Hassan said she had it in a safe-deposit box in her bank."

"How did you know she had it, George?"

"Because as soon as we hatched this plot, I had all the phones in my area bugged. I heard her call that reporter, so I sent Hassan after her to get it back and silence her," George Saxton responded.

* * *

The next day, most of the personnel in the FBI building were back to work. Clive was holding a meeting with the forensic team in his office, with Dan and Mike Clancy, the chief of the forensic department, who spoke up. "Mr. Banner, the team spent all day yesterday and long into the night along with the fire department arson team. We think we have found parts of the vehicle that brought the bomb into the garage."

"It was brought in by a vehicle? How did it get past our guard?" asked Banner.

"We interviewed the guard in the hospital. He's injured, but not seriously. He said he remembers a van going into the garage about half an hour before the blast. The driver had an e-mail from your office manager to come and fix the plumbing. He said he looked into the back of the van but just saw plumbing tools. That was the only van or truck that came into the garage that day."

"Are you sure that was the van that carried the bomb?"

"It would have to be. A bomb that would do that much damage would be too large to carry in a car. We talked to Muriel, your office manager, and she said she never sent an email to anyone to fix the plumbing. She has your maintenance department do that kind of work."

"You said you have found parts of the vehicle that carried the bomb. How do you know that it was that vehicle? Weren't other cars blown apart?"

"No. Most of the cars that surrounded the van were badly mangled by the blast. Some were crushed and lost some parts but essentially stayed intact. The blast from inside the van just blew it apart and into small pieces, but the heavier parts, like the rear axle and frame, were twisted but remained intact. We were able to get the VIN from the axle, and we found the VIN tag from the dashboard. The van was a Dodge. We are checking with Chrysler Corporation to see whom the van was sold to."

"What was the bomb made of?" Clive asked.

"Our lab found traces of ammonium nitrate off the cars and the ceiling of the garage as well as nitromethane. The same kind of a bomb used in the Oklahoma City bombing. I'm sending agents out today to find out who purchased these materials in the last month. When Chrysler tells me whom they sold the van to, we'll follow up. Mr. Banner, I think we will find out who bombed this building."

"That's fine, gentlemen. Good work. Keep me informed. When Chrysler tells you who purchased the van, let me know. I want Dan Morris to get involved in the case."

* * *

Carol was anxious to find out any new evidence in the FBI building bombing, so she called Dan Morris. "Dan, my editor is anxious to go to print with anything new the bureau has on the bombing of your building. Anything you can tell me?"

"We will be having a press conference this afternoon. You can get all the findings then."

"But, Dan, that will be too late for our afternoon edition. Can't you tell me now? The paper won't be on the street until after you hold your conference."

"Okay, Carol, but keep it under your hat where you got the info from. I'm getting a feeling that sleeping with you will get me in a lot of hot water."

"You never know, Dan, when you might get the chance again."

"Do I detect a hope in your comment?"

"We'll see, Dan, we'll see. Now give me the latest," Carol, teasing a little bit.

"Okay, forensics found out that it was a van that brought the explosives into the garage. We found the rear axle and part of the dashboard from the van, from which we got the VIN. The van was made by Chrysler. We sent them an e-mail asking them who bought the van. When we get that, we will find the culprit."

"Is anyone missing from your building?"

"No. Everyone is accounted for. There were no deaths, but forty-one people went to the hospital. Some are in critical condition. That's it, Carol. When we get the owner of the van from Chrysler, I'll let you know."

"What about this Hassan fellow? Anything new?"

"No. That's on hold until we get this bomber found."

***

Chrysler came back with an e-mail. It said the van was sold to Handy Car Rental Agency at the Reagan International Airport. It was two years old and was painted yellow. When Clive read the e-mail, he called Dan. "I just read the e-mail from Chrysler. They said the van used in the bombing was sold to the Handy Car Rental Agency at the airport. Get on it, Dan. Find out who rented the van."

Dan went into the office of the Handy Car Rental Agency. The young man behind the counter asked, "Can I help you, sir?"

Dan showed the clerk his FBI badge and credentials. "Yes. I need some information on one of your clients."

"Yes, sir. What's his name?"

"I don't know. I want you to tell me."

"Without his name, I can't help you," the man said.

"I have the VIN of the yellow van he rented from you."

"Oh, that's different. Give me the number."

The clerk typed in the VIN into his computer. In a few seconds, he said, "Yes, a Mr. Peter Harmon rented the van five days ago."

"Do you have his address?"

"Yes, sir."

"Who rented the van to him?"

The clerk looked at his computer. "I did, sir."

"Do you remember what he looked like?"

"Let me think . . . Harmon . . . Harmon. Oh yes, I remember. He had dark skin but an American name. I mentioned that to him, and he said he had an American father but an Arab mother."

"Can you describe him?"

"I can do better than that. Our policy is to copy the driver's license of all our clients when they rent from us."

"Wonderful! Can I see it?"

The man said, delighted, "Certainly."

The clerk went to a file, pulled out a folder, and handed it to Dan. Hassan's driver's license was there. He looked at it and smiled. Then he asked the clerk, "How did he pay?"

"Well, he hasn't yet. He will pay when he returns the van."

"Don't you take a deposit or a credit card?"

"Yes. I have his credit card number."

"Let me have it."

"Let me make a copy of both the license and credit card number for you."

Dan said, "Okay. By the way, your van won't be returned."

"Oh? How come?"

"It was in the garage of our building when the bomb went off. It's destroyed."

The clerk looked at the rental agreement with Hassan. "Well, I see Mr. Harmon had insurance. So he's okay."

Dan left and went back to his office. He sat down and looked at the picture on Peter Harmon's driver's license and thought, *An American father and an Arab mother? Why does he have dark skin?* He studied the picture some more then thought, *If he had dark hair and no beard, I'd bet he would look like Hassan, the killer.*

Dan went to the sketch artist. "Henry, I have a photo here of a man with blond hair and a red beard. I think the hair and beard are phony. Can you remove the hair on his head and face and put a black widow's peak on his head?"

"Sure. I have to put it in the computer."

Henry copied the picture, and it appeared on his screen. "Now what did you want to do?"

"Take out his blond hair."

Henry punched a few keys and drew the curser across the picture's head and chin. "There. What else?"

"Give him black hair with a widow's peak coming over his forehead."

Again, Henry typed in some data and moved his curser over the head of the picture. "How's that, Dan?"

"That's perfect. Now print that. Then I want to add something else."

After the picture was printed, Dan said, "Okay, now give the face a thin black mustache and a small black goatee."

Henry typed in some data then moved his curser over the upper lip and the chin on the picture. "Is that what you want?" asked Henry.

"You bet. Now print that, and keep that picture in your files and call it Hassan."

"Okay, Dan. You're the boss."

Dan took the pictures back to his desk. He took out the file on Hassan and took out the pictures from Interpol and the artist's sketch of the man seen in the hospital. He smiled broadly and said to himself, *Gotcha.*

He called the credit card company that Hassan had given the clerk at the car rental agency. He told them he was from the FBI, gave them his badge number, the credit card number, and the name on the credit card, and asked if they had an address for Peter Harmon. The clerk came back and gave Dan an address in Somerset, a town just north of Washington, DC.

He hung up the phone, sat back in his chair, and mused to himself, *That, Mr. Hassan, is your first and fatal mistake.*

Dan took the partner he was working with and went to see Clive Banner. "What have you got, Dan? Anything?" Clive asked.

"Yep. I know who set off the bomb in our garage."

"You do? Who?"

Dan exclaimed, "Hassan Kahil!"

"The one we thought killed the Bigelows and that Patricia girl and Saxton's aide?"

"One and the same."

"What brought you to that conclusion?"

"Remember the nurse at the hospital where Jerry Baldwin was murdered?"

"Yes. What about her? How is she tied to this bombing?"

"Give me a minute, Chief, and I'll tie it all together for you."

"Okay, Dan, go ahead."

"That nurse gave our artist a description of the man she saw in the hospital, a man she had never seen before. We sent that composite to Interpol, and they identified the man as Hassan Kahil. When the VIN was found in the wreckage in the garage and identified the van as a Dodge, we got Chrysler to tell us where that van was sold. It turned out to be a rental agency at the airport here in town. They rented it to a man named Peter Harmon, a dark-skinned man with blond hair and a blond beard. They had a copy of his driver's license and credit card. I thought the dark skin and blond hair didn't fit together, so I took the picture to our sketch artist and had him put it in the computer. He took off the blond hair and beard and replaced it with black hair and a small mustache and goatee, and this was the result."

Dan handed Clive the new composite. "So?" he said as he looked at it.

"Here," Dan said, "take a look at the photo from Interpol. Compare them."

Clive looked at both of them then turned to Dan and said, "They are the same man."

"Precisely," said Dan. "This is the man who set off the bomb in our garage and the same man who shot Jerry Baldwin. And I'll bet he murdered the Bigelows and Patricia Manning. He's the one who didn't want that folder of Eagle Down to become public."

"So what does he have to gain from all this?"

"Nothing, I suppose, except he's a hired killer earning his pay."

"Now the big question: whom is he working for?"

"That, I don't know. But I have my suspicions," Dan said.

"And who might that be?"

"George Saxton."

"Why him?"

"He and Samuel Giddings have the most to gain if the president and vice president are killed."

"That's not enough to accuse him."

"No, but that phone call the morning of the bombing—when someone said 'I'm ready. Today is the time,' and Saxton replied, 'No killing'—tells me Hassan called Saxton and told him he was going to set off the bomb. We could get a voice comparison of Hassan's voice if we had him in lockup. Saxton would be a cinch since he makes speeches all the time."

"One important question: do you know where Hassan is?"

"The credit card company gave me an address in Somerset, just a few miles from here. I was planning to see if he is there."

"No, Dan. If Hassan is at that address, I want him alive. We, the local police, and a SWAT team should go after him. The way he killed those people without mercy means he is a savage killer and may not want to be taken alive."

"Do you want me to get in touch with the locals?"

"No, Dan. I'll do that. I want you in on this. Do you have a composite of what Hassan would look like without his hair?"

"No, but I can get one. Why do you want it?"

"I want every policeman in on this capture to know what Hassan looks like. I don't want him to get away or injure some innocent person."

"I'll have Henry make up the picture from the Interpol picture. He has it in his computer, and all he has to do is remove the hair from the picture."

Clive called the local police and arranged to meet them at Hassan's address along with a SWAT team. When Dan came back with the pictures, Clive, Dan, and four other agents left for Somerset. When they got to the address, the local police and a SWAT team were already there. Clive found the chief of the local police force.

"Hello, Chief. I'm Clive Banner, head of the FBI," he said.

"Yes. I recognize you from your pictures in the paper. What have we got here that it requires this much force?"

"A very dangerous man. He's killed four people we know of, and he's wanted by Interpol for assassinations in Europe. His name is Hassan Kahil. He is also in on an attempt to assassinate the president. Here is his picture. Make sure all your men see it. I want this bastard alive. He's the one who bombed our building."

"My, this guy has been busy. Okay, I'll pass this photo around. Do you know what unit he's in?"

"Yes, 2C on the second floor."

"Okay, I'll have my men evacuate the other people in the building."

The local police went to every apartment in the building and asked the tenants to leave. Hassan was watching TV and had no idea that the police and FBI were surrounding the building. In a short time, all the tenants were out of the building. SWAT men were outside Hassan's door, down in front, and in the back of the building in case Hassan tried to get out his back window and escape down the alley. When all the men were ready, they signaled the chief. "Okay, Mr. Banner, the men are in position."

Clive spoke into his bullhorn. "hassan, hassan kahil, this is the fbi. we have you surrounded. you are under arrest. give up and come out with your hands up. do not carry any weapons!"

When Hassan heard the bullhorn, he jumped up, ran to the front window, and looked out. In the street in front of his apartment, he could see a dozen or more police vehicles and a SWAT van. He swore, "Goddamn it! How in hell did they find me?"

He immediately picked up his cell phone and called Senator Saxton. Saxton answered, "Yes?"

"This is Hassan. The FBI is outside. Did you tell them where I live?"

"Of course not! Why would I do a dumb thing like that?"

"Well, someone did. How else would they know where I live?"

"I don't know. You must have left a clue at one of the murder scenes or when you bombed the FBI building."

"No. I am always very careful."

"Can you get away?" Saxton asked.

"No. I don't think so. They say they have the building surrounded, and they have many cars out front."

"Well, if they take you, keep your mouth shut. I'll see you get a good lawyer."

"And what good will that do? I'm wanted in Europe as well as here."

"Take one thing at a time. If the Ghost does his thing, we will be in a position to help you. Giddings, as president, can pardon you if they convict you. So sit tight and keep quiet." Then he hung up.

Hassan heard the bullhorn again. "hassan, you have not answered me. are you going to surrender, or are we going to have to take you by force?"

Hassan went to the closet and got his AK-47. He broke the front window with the barrel and shot off numerous rounds, spraying the bullets all over the police cars, where the police were hiding.

Clive signaled the chief to let the tear gas go. Ten rounds of tear gas exploded into the front and back windows of Hassan's apartment. In a short time, the apartment was filled with tear gas. Hassan put his handkerchief to his mouth and nose, but he couldn't breathe. His lungs were filled with tear gas, and his eyes burned, so he couldn't see. He began to cough violently to clear his lungs. When the SWAT men outside his door heard his coughing, they knew he couldn't see, so they used a ram and busted in his door. They wore gas masks with glass covering their eyes. They saw Hassan in the middle of the room, coughing, with the AK-47 in one hand and his handkerchief in the other. Two men grabbed Hassan and pushed him to the floor, while another man grabbed the AK-47 from his hand. One man sat on Hassan, while the other cuffed his hands behind his back. Hassan was still coughing violently, and he couldn't see.

His eyes were filled with tears. One of the SWAT men went out the door and signaled Clive and the chief that Hassan was in custody.

Clive, the chief, and Dan came into the apartment. Hassan was sitting on the couch, still coughing and with tears running down his face. Clive walked over to him, put his hand under Hassan's chin, lifted his face, and said in an angry voice, "You son of a bitch! You are going to pay for blowing up my building! Why did you do it?"

Hassan couldn't see and was still trying to clear his lungs, so he just shook his head back and forth. Clive turned to Dan, who was behind him. "Search this place with a fine-tooth comb. There's got to be evidence in here."

"Yes, sir," said Dan.

Clive said to the chief, "I want this man in a federal lockup, Chief. Take him in to Washington."

Dan didn't have to look far. Sitting on the kitchen table was a briefcase. When he opened it up, he found three passports in different names; three driver's licenses with the same names as the passports; hair, glasses, and fake beards and mustaches that matched the pictures on the documents; and a checkbook for a Swiss bank account.

"Good grief! This guy is a chameleon. He has a disguise for any eventuality."

Then he found two automatics in the dresser drawer. "Well, what do we have here? A Berretta and a Glock. I'll bet they match the slugs taken from the Bigelows, Patricia, and Jerry Baldwin." Then he said to one of the officers watching Hassan, "Stand him up. I want to search him."

Dan found keys, a wallet, and a cell phone. "Looks like you have been using your phone a lot, Hassan. A lot of calls to this number. Who is it?" he asked, showing the phone to Hassan.

Hassan never said a word. He just glared at Dan.

"That's okay. We can get a record of your calls from the phone service you use," Dan said.

* * *

Later that day, Dan sat in Clive's office. "Did you find any evidence in Hassan's apartment, Dan?" asked Clive.

"Yes. I found two guns I believe were used in the killings of the Bigelows, Patricia Manning, and Jerry Baldwin. I turned them over to ballistics for testing. I'm sure they will be a match."

"Anything else?" Clive asked.

"Yes. Sales receipts for ammonium nitrate bought at several fertilizer stores and the purchase of a fifty-five-gallon drum of nitromethane. He also bought parts at an electronics store. My guess is he used them to make a detonator and timer for the bomb. The guard at the garage can testify that he let the van in the garage and will identify Hassan in disguise. I contacted the phone company he used for his cell phone and asked them for a record of his phone calls. He seems to have called one number a lot. Finally, he had a briefcase that had three sets of disguises and phony passports and driver's licenses in it. I don't know which identity he used to get into this country, but I'm having immigration check that out. With the sales receipts and the testimony of the clerk at the car rental company and the guard, I think we have enough to charge him with the bombing of this building."

"What about the murders?"

"All we have, if it turns out the slugs from the victims match the guns. We need a motive for the killings."

"What about keeping the plot of Eagle Down from becoming public?"

"We have no way to link him to that. If his phone calls are to the perpetrators of the plot, that may be helpful. One other thing, Chief, can we prove there is a plot? Anyone can claim that that document was a gag or someone's fantasy. After all, no one has seen this

Ghost fellow. Interpol has no ID on him. A good defense lawyer can sway a jury on that one without any trouble."

"True. Let's work on Hassan. Has he asked for a lawyer yet?" Clive said.

"No. No one has interrogated him yet. I read him his rights just before he was taken to lockup. With your permission, I would like to interrogate him."

"Fine, except get the justice department involved. Get one of their attorneys from the attorney general's office to sit with you when you talk to Hassan. I want no screwup on the interrogation."

"Will do. One more thing, what can I release to the press? Remember, we promised Sam Corcoran, the editor of the *Washington Ledger*, an exclusive on this story."

"Okay, call him and give him the capture of Hassan and the fact that he is our chief suspect in the murders and the bombing of this building. Don't release anything on the Eagle Down plot. We have to find the men behind that, and I don't want the public alarmed about the safety of the president," Clive finished.

* * *

When Dan left Clive's office, he called Carol. "Carol, you'll be happy to know we have captured the killer of the Bigelows and the other two victims. We also are charging him with bombing the FBI building. I would like to come over to your office and tell you what we are going to release in a press conference this afternoon."

"Can we print it?"

"Yes. We promised you an exclusive, didn't we? But nothing yet on the Eagle Down plot."

"Great. Dan, I'll go tell Sam."

"Okay. I'll be there in fifteen minutes."

* * *

Dan sat in Sam's office with Sam, Carol, and Bob and gave them the complete story on Hassan and his capture. When he finished, he commented, "Mr. Banner does not want the story of Eagle Down to be released to the public for two reasons. One, he doesn't want the public scared about our president being killed, and two, he doesn't want the planners of the plot to be aware that we know about it until we catch the Ghost or foil his plot, whenever it may be."

The afternoon edition of the *Washington Ledger* hit the streets with this banner headline: murderer-bomber caught. The paper carried the entire story of Hassan's murders and his bombing of the FBI building.

Clive Banner got an appointment with president Gerald Harrison before the paper was released on the street. Paul Barrows also attended the meeting.

"Okay, Clive, you called the meeting. Let's hear it. Is it about the attempt on my life?" the president asked.

"Yes and no."

"Well, let's hear the yes part first."

"Okay. We caught the fellow named Hassan Kahil."

"The one you thought murdered Harry and his wife?"

"Yes. And also that Patricia woman in Chantilly and George Saxton's aide. We searched his apartment and found two guns, a Berretta and a Glock. The slugs from the murder victims came from those two guns. So that should satisfy both you and Paul here. We found Harry's killer. Hassan is the killer. We also have strong evidence that this Hassan character set off the bomb in our building. So far, he's been in lockup. We haven't interrogated him yet. We hope to get the names of the men behind the plot to assassinate you from him."

"What about this Ghost character? Anything on him?" Gerald asked.

"No. But CIA and Interpol think he's in this country. The Eagle Down plan says to assassinate you to stop your stimulus bill from going to a vote. From what I gather from the newspapers, that vote isn't far off. So they expect the Ghost to make his move soon."

"Any idea how he plans to assassinate me?"

"No. Interpol says he has used a variety of methods in the past depending on the victim's habits, speaking engagements, and travel plans. Timothy Hendricks, your head of Secret Service, says he has every possible avenue covered. He feels confident he can protect you no matter what," Clive said.

"Do you think this Hassan fellow knows anything about the Ghost?"

"Can't tell. They are in the same line of work, assassinations, but the Ghost is considered the top man in his profession. We, of course, will try to get everything we can when we interrogate Hassan. If we get anything, I'll let Timothy and you know."

The president said, "Okay, Clive. Thanks for the update."

* * *

When Clive got back to his office, he called Dan in. "Sit down, Dan. I just updated the president where we are on Hassan and the Ghost. Have you contacted the attorney general's office yet to get a prosecutor to attend the interrogation of Hassan?"

"Yes. They are sending Ron Carter, their top man."

"Good. Okay, get him to the lockup. I want Hassan interrogated right away. He may know the plans of the Ghost. If he does, we can lay a trap for that son of a bitch."

"Okay, Chief. I'll call Carter right away."

* * *

When Ron Carter arrived at the jail, he introduced himself to Dan. Dan explained to Ron, "This man—Hassan, as you probably have read—is a killer of four people we know of. He's the one, according to our evidence, who set off the bomb in the FBI building. Now we feel we have enough evidence to convict him. We are after two things: one, who is behind a plot to kill the president—"

"There's a plot to kill the president?" Ron said, interrupting Dan.

"Yes, and you must keep that to yourself. That's number 2. There is an assassin in this country from Europe or Asia who was hired by a man or group of men who don't want the president's stimulus bill passed and who are planning on assassinating him to stop the bill from becoming law. He goes by the name of the Ghost."

"Ghost? That's a strange name for a killer."

"Interpol gave him that name because no one knows what he looks like. He kills and fades into obscurity. What we are hoping is Hassan can identify him and we can stop him before he tries to kill the president."

"Okay, Dan, I got the picture."

Dan and Ron were sitting at a table in the interrogation room when Hassan was led in. He had a chain around his waist, handcuffs that were attached to the chain, and a long chain going from the chain on his waist to a chain around his ankles. The guard led him to the table and then backed off to stand against the wall and watch Hassan.

"Sit down, Hassan," said Dan.

Hassan sat down with a frown on his face and looked at both men.

"I'm Agent Dan Morris from the FBI, and this is Ron Carter from the attorney general's office. We know what crimes you have committed, and we want you to verify what we've found. I'm going to read you your rights, again." Then Dan read from a card and put it away in his pocket.

"You mean you want me to confess?" Hassan said.

"Yes. That would save everyone a lot of time."

"As I understand, your code of justice here in this country is I am innocent and you have to prove me guilty. Is that not correct?"

"Yes, that's correct. But we have substantial evidence against you, and proving that will be easy."

"Then why are you here? Am I not entitled to an attorney?"

"Yes, and if you ask for one, the court will assign one to you. Now, tell me, who is behind the plot to kill our president?" Dan asked.

"I don't know what you are talking about."

"Come now, Hassan. Isn't the reason you murdered four people to keep the plot a secret?"

"I didn't murder anyone. You have me confused with someone else."

"That's not what the evidence says."

Hassan asked, "What evidence?"

"We found two guns in your apartment, a Berretta and a Glock. The bullets taken from the murder victims came from those guns."

"You planted those guns there. They don't belong to me."

"Then why do they have your fingerprints on them?"

"I have no idea."

"Okay, let's talk about your Mercedes, which we found in the garage at your apartment."

"What about it?"

"We found paint on the side of your car, which was damaged, that is a perfect match with the car of the two reporters you pushed off the road."

"Coincidence. Many cars have the same paint."

"Look, Hassan, you killed the Bigelows because of an email he sent to George Saxton and Admiral Goodman. Someone told you to kill them to keep him from making any more inquiries about Eagle Down. Who was that?"

"Never heard of Eagle Down."

"Then you killed a woman, Patricia Manning, because she had a copy of the plan, and you wrecked her apartment to find it, but she had it in a safe-deposit box. Who told you to murder her?"

"I told you, I know nothing of this plan."

"Then when two reporters came close to getting Jerry Baldwin to tell them about the plan, you tried to murder him by shooting him and running him off the road, but you failed. So the next day, you went to the hospital and shot him. But a woman saw you and can identify you. Hassan, we have evidence to send you to prison for life or execute you. Or we could turn you over to Interpol. They will send you to some of the Far Eastern countries where you murdered people, and you can be executed by them or spend the rest of your life in their miserable prisons."

"This is your fairy tale. You have to prove it."

"Hassan, I just told you what evidence we have. Ron, tell him what will happen."

Ron looked at Hassan and said, "First, you will be arraigned in court then go to trial. Let me assure you that with the evidence that Dan has told you about, I will have no trouble convincing a jury to convict you. I will ask for the death penalty and will get it."

"Maybe if I have a good lawyer, he will convince the jury that I am innocent."

"I don't think so. The evidence is too strong."

"Now, Hassan," Dan said, "let's talk about the bombing of the FBI building. We know it was you, but we don't know why. What was your motive? As far as we can tell, it had nothing to do with the Eagle Down plot."

"I had nothing to do with that bombing, absolutely nothing."

"I beg to differ with you. All the evidence points to you."

Hassan asked, "What evidence?"

"You rented the van that had the explosives in it. The clerk at the car rental agency can identify you. He made a copy of your phony driver's license and your credit card. We found receipts for your purchases of ammonium nitrate and nitromethane and parts for a detonator in your apartment, and the guard at the gate to the garage will identify you. That's more evidence than what convicted Timothy McVeigh for the Oklahoma City bombing. No, Hassan, we have you solid on that one. The one mistake you made was giving the credit card company your address. Make it easy on yourself and tell us who was behind the plot, and maybe we can take the death penalty off the table."

"I told you before, and I will tell you again, I had nothing to do with those murders or that bombing, and I have nothing more to say. I want a lawyer. As you said, it's my right."

"Okay, Hassan, if that's the way you want to play it, but, my friend, you are going to have a needle in your arm to send you to your eternity."

Dan waved the guard over to take Hassan back to his cell.

When the guard escorted Hassan out of the room, Dan asked Ron, "What do you think, Ron? Will he crack?"

"I doubt it. He didn't ask us to get him a lawyer, so I expect he will hire his own. I'll bet he has the money to do it. He's been killing for money, so he probably has plenty of cash. Incidentally, do you have any idea who is behind this plot to kill the president?"

"Yes, but it's just a theory. We don't want to move on it until we have some concrete evidence. I'm sorry I cannot reveal that."

"That's okay. Just for your information, the attorney general gave me this case. So if anything new comes up, get it to me. I will have Hassan arraigned the day after tomorrow," Ron responded.

* * *

Hassan requested he make a phone call, and his request was granted. He phoned George Saxton. When Saxton answered the phone, Hassan said, "I am in the jail in Washington. You promised me a top-flight lawyer. Where is he?"

"Be patient. I contacted a man from Chicago. He will be here tomorrow. His name is Austin McGregor. He is one of the best defense lawyers in the country. As soon as he arrives, he will see you. Have they interrogated you yet?"

"Yes, just a while ago. A man from the FBI and someone from the justice department."

"Did you tell them anything?"

"No. I just denied everything. They have some evidence about the killings and the bombing, but I told them nothing."

"Call me if you need something, but be careful. Don't let anyone know whom you call."

Hassan hung up, and Saxton went to Sam Giddings's office to update him.

CHAPTER 8

Dan sat in Clive Banner's office. "Chief, the interrogation went nowhere. He denied everything, even after I told him of the evidence we had. He lawyered up and refused to talk anymore."

"Did you read him his rights?" asked Clive.

"Yes, before I began to question him. Ron witnessed that."

"Good. Now, about getting him a lawyer, I'll call justice and see what we can do."

Later, Clive called Charles Meyer, the attorney general. "Chuck, we need a defense attorney for a man named Hassan Kahil."

"Isn't he the one you arrested for killing those four people and bombing your building?"

"Yes."

"I suppose we'd better give him the best we have. This will be a high-profile case, and we don't want it said we didn't give him a fair trial. Was he read his rights?"

"Yep."

"Any chance he would roll on his employer?"

"No. Dan Morris interrogated him and said he denied everything and said no one hired him. Dan even mentioned he might take the death penalty off the table if he gave up the people who hired him, but he just denied everything. When you take a look at the evidence we have against him, you'll see this case will be a slam dunk."

"I hope you're right. You never know what a jury will do. In my career, I have been surprised a number of times."

* * *

The next morning, Hassan was led out of his cell to an interrogation room. When he walked in, there was a man sitting there. He appeared to be in his late fifties, had a full head of graying hair, and wore dark-rimmed glasses.

As Hassan walked in, the man stood up and reached out to shake his hand. "How do you do, Mr. Kahil? I'm Austin McGregor, your attorney. I was retained by Senator Saxton."

Hassan shook his hand and took notice that McGregor was a rather tall man and quite slim. As he sat down, McGregor asked, "Are you being treated fairly, Mr. Kahil?"

"Yes. Tell me, are you a good lawyer?"

"I'm considered one of the best in the country, if I believe what I hear. Why are you concerned?"

"The FBI was in here yesterday and quizzed me and told me the evidence they have against me."

"I haven't seen the prosecutor yet, so I can't make any judgments. We go through a process known as discovery. That's when the prosecution is required by law to disclose any and all evidence they have to the defense, even exculpatory evidence."

"What's that?" Hassan asked.

"Evidence that might show your innocence."

"So why are you here?"

"I wanted to meet my client and get your side of the story. As I understand it from Senator Saxton, you are charged with four murders and bombing a federal building. Is that correct?"

"That's what they say."

"Is all or any part of those charges true?"

"You are supposed to be my lawyer, and right off the bat, you want me to confess."

"No, Mr. Kahil. I just wanted to find out what I'm up against. I always consider my clients innocent. I never ask them if they are guilty. Sometimes a client will have committed a crime but has extenuating circumstances, which could result in a guilty plea for a lesser sentence."

"Well, I'm telling you, I did not commit those murders or blow up that building. Now can you get me off?"

"Before I can answer that, I have to see what the evidence against you is. If you are innocent, then I'm sure you stand a good chance of going free. What have you told the police?"

"Nothing. Absolutely nothing. They grilled me, but I denied everything."

"Good. Say nothing to them. They are required to have your attorney with you if they want to talk to you. I will be back. I will get in touch with the federal prosecutor's office and ask for a discovery. So just sit tight," McGregor said.

* * *

Gerald Harrison was sitting in the oval office when his chief of staff, Paul Barrows, came in. "Mr. President, the vice president would like to see you."

"Sure, Paul. What is it about?"

"Your trip tomorrow to Detroit."

"Okay, have her come in," the president said.

Grace Arden walked in and was invited to sit down on the couch. She was an attractive woman in her midfifties. Her hair had not grayed as yet. She had a handsome face and still had her girlish figure. She was a governor before Harrison asked her to join his ticket.

Harrison smiled at her as he sat down alongside her. "What can I do for you today, Grace?" he asked.

"It's about your trip tomorrow to Detroit. I would like to beg off."

"Oh. Has something come up? Your presence at these hometown meetings is always appreciated by the people. You are very popular."

"I know, and I hate to disappoint you, but one of my grandchildren was injured and is in critical condition in the hospital, and my daughter is beside herself. She needs my support."

"By all means, Grace, stay and help her. I can handle the rally by myself. We only have a few more trips, I hope, and maybe we can force a vote on my bill."

* * *

Abdul had been waiting for this trip by the president. Detroit was near the Canadian border, and the president and vice president would be on Air Force One. So he and the pilot checked and rechecked the jet and went over and over the procedure to arm and fire the missile. He knew he had to get in close to ensure a hit to bring the big Boeing 747 down. He was not aware that Grace Arden would not be on the flight since that was a last-minute decision. He had picked that flight so he could fulfill his contract to kill the president and vice president together. If he killed just one, then the second would have tighter security, and it would be impossible to take out the second target.

He chose Detroit because after destroying Air Force One, he could drop down to treetop level and be over Lake Huron in a very short time, thus avoiding Detroit center radar. If they did pick him up on their radar, he would appear as a normal VFR flight. Then he could fly over Lake Huron just fifty feet above the water and be hidden from radar and fly VFR into Sault Ste. Marie in Canada. There, he could contact the tower and file an IFR flight plan (instrument flight rules) out of Canada. If NORAD (North American Aerospace Defense Command) did pick him up and send fighters, they could not enter Canadian airspace. He thought it was the perfect plan.

Air Force One would land at Wright Patterson Air Force Base, and the president and vice president would take their helicopter to Detroit. Abdul planned to fly VFR at seventeen thousand feet. FAA rules do not allow VFR flights above eighteen thousand feet, so he would stay at seventeen thousand feet until he was near Air Force One, which would be descending for a landing at Wright Patterson Air Force Base. That way, he could avoid being tracked by air traffic control, which tracked every plane flying IFR above eighteen thousand feet. But VFR flights just transmitted their altitude and squawked twelve hundred from their transponder on the radar screen. Only when the Citation jet was within ten miles of the Boeing 747 would air traffic control be alarmed and warn Air Force One that there was traffic nearby. Since the Cessna Citation X jet could reach airspeed of six hundred miles an hour, it would be too late for Air Force One to escape. Abdul had planned out this strategy long before buying the Iranian air-to-air missile and having the equipment installed. It had been expensive but worth it. The Citation was fueled, the missile was loaded onto its underwing cradle hard-point, and the jet was ready to go but still hidden in the hangar to avoid public scrutiny.

* * *

The president was up early and took his helicopter, *Marine One*, to Andrews Air Force Base, where Air Force One was based and maintained by the presidential airlift group. The plane was made ready and checked and double-checked to see if all systems were functioning. Before the president arrived, a contingent of the traveling press, Secret Service, and senior advisers to the president came on board. No other guests were to travel with the president that day. When he was on board, he went to the cockpit and greeted the pilot and copilot then went back to his lounge. The 747 received clearance for takeoff, roared down the runway, and headed for Wright Patterson Air Base near Dayton, Ohio.

Abdul knew when the president would arrive at Detroit, so he calculated when the helicopter would take the president to Detroit and then when Air Force One would land. He planned to take off early in the morning to be sure to get to Wright Patterson before Air Force One. He and the pilot opened the hangar doors and rolled the Citation jet out. After the cockpit preflight check, they started the engines and called the tower for permission to taxi to the runway. They received permission to take off.

As the jet rolled down the runway, one of the controllers in the tower said to the other, "Do you see that Citation taking off? It looked like it had a missile under its wing."

The other controller picked up his binoculars and followed the jet down the runway until it left the ground. He turned to his partner and commented, "Yeah, that looked like a missile. What would a private jet be doing with a missile? I've never seen or heard of that before."

"It must be experimental."

So neither man reported it to the FAA. Abdul had successfully hidden the modified jet and left the ground without being questioned or investigated. He was now in the air, heading for a rendezvous with Air Force One.

* * *

That same morning, Austin McGregor arrived at Ron Carter's office. After the usual handshaking and introductions, Ron asked, "How can Hassan afford such a high-priced attorney? Is someone else paying for your services?"

"Now, Mr. Carter, you know that's privileged information."

"I know, but at least I tried. You see, Hassan is hiding who financed and paid him to commit those murders and blow up the FBI building."

"That, Mr. Carter, has not been established."

"Well, I have enough evidence on my hands that says he did commit those crimes, and I'll share it with you before the formal discovery."

"Fine. That's what I'm here for."

"What began this series of murders was an e-mail sent by the assistant chief of staff for the president to two men, Senator Saxton and Admiral Goodman. The e-mail asked about a project called Eagle Down. Both men claim they've never heard of it, yet that very night, that man and his wife were murdered in their bed. Right after that, a woman claimed to have a copy of that plan, and she was murdered. Then an aide to Senator Saxton was murdered. A nurse in the hospital will identify Hassan, who was in the hospital at the time Saxton's aide was murdered. When we searched Hassan's apartment—and yes, we had a search warrant—we found the two guns used in the murders. They had Hassan's fingerprints on them. The bullets removed from the victims came from those two guns. That ties him in as the murderer. Now to the bombing. We have the clerk who rented the van used in the bombing. He will identify Hassan as the man who rented the van. We have sales slips for the material used in the bombing found in Hassan's apartment. He used his credit card. We have the guard at the gate who let Hassan into the underground garage. He will ID Hassan. We have more, but that should give you an idea what you'll be up against."

"Mr. Carter, on the surface, it sounds formidable. But as you will see, we will challenge every one of those items."

"But it won't do you any good. Most of the scientific items, like ballistics and fingerprints, can't be challenged. Your client gave no reason for bombing the building. I'm going to charge your client with a terrorist act, and him being of Arab decent, he will be convicted."

"All right, Mr. Carter, I'm making a formal request for discovery. When can I expect your evidence, names of witnesses, and what they will testify to?"

"I'll have it to you the day after tomorrow. Is that satisfactory?"

"Yes."

"Where are you staying?"

"At the Marriott," McGregor said.

"Fine. I'll have a messenger deliver it to you."

* * *

Abdul flew the Citation at maximum speed at flight level 35. When he got near Wright Patterson, he canceled his IFR flight, went on VFR, dropped down to seventeen thousand feet, and squawked twelve hundred from his transponder. He was no longer tracked by air traffic control; he was simply on their radar. He flew a fifty-mile circle around Wright Patterson Air Force Base, watching his radar for the Boeing 747 to appear on his screen. He dropped his airspeed to two hundred and fifty knots and waited.

When Air Force One was within fifty miles of Wright Patterson Air Base, Colonel Elkhart, the pilot, radioed Wright Patterson approach, who requested him to descend to fifteen thousand feet. It was then that Abdul saw the Boeing 747 on his radar screen. The 747 was twenty-five miles to his left and flying in the opposite direction. He pushed the throttles forward to achieve maximum speed and banked left, heading toward the 747. Air Force One was descending through twenty thousand feet when the Citation was within twenty miles.

A Wright Patterson radar operator saw the Citation approaching the 747. He turned to another operator sitting next to him. "I got a VFR plane approaching Air Force One. He's heading directly for him. He's going at high speed and descending to the same altitude as Air Force One."

The other operator said, "Yes, I see him. Get Air Force One out of there."

The radar operator radioed Air Force One. "Air Force One, this is Wright Patterson approach. You have a bogie heading right for you. Turn ninety degrees right and climb to twenty thousand."

Then, on the same frequency, he called the Citation jet. "Unidentified jet twenty miles east of Wright Patterson at nineteen thousand feet on VFR, this is Wright Patterson approach. Turn left ninety degrees and descend to sixteen thousand feet."

Abdul had his radio tuned to the Wright Patterson approach frequency and heard the instructions from Wright Patterson approach, but he just ignored them. He was interested in what instructions Wright Patterson approach would give the 747. He pulled up and started to climb to twenty thousand feet, where the 747 was. When the operator saw the Citation jet climb, he called his supervisor. "Boss, I got a jet chasing Air Force One. He ignored my instructions to descend and is heading for Air Force One."

"How do you know it's a jet?"

"His speed. No prop plane can go that fast. Look how fast he is closing in on the 747."

"I see. He's just ten miles behind him. Get Air Force One to maneuver down to a lower level, quick. I'll scramble two F-16s that are on the ready line."

The supervisor pushed a button, and a Klaxon horn blared in the pilot's ready room. The supervisor picked up a mike and said, "Ready, pilots. Man your planes."

Two pilots waiting in a ready room heard the call, jumped up, and ran to the F-16s waiting just off the taxiway. The jets had been preflight checked and were ready to fly. They had six missiles each as well as the M61 Vulcan cannon. They got into the jets, fixed their seat belts, put on their helmets and oxygen masks, and started the engines. They called the tower and were given instructions to taxi to the runway. As they taxied, the tower radioed them and said, "Ready flight, you are cleared for takeoff. Your call sign is Arrow."

"Cleared for takeoff, call sign Arrow. Roger," replied the lead pilot.

When the two jets reached the runway, they thundered down at full throttle and radioed, "Arrow flight rolling."

When they were airborne, the tower gave them instructions. "Arrow flight, there is a bogie at twenty thousand chasing Air Force One. Your heading is ninety degrees. Intercept the bogie and force him to land."

Abdul reached twenty thousand feet and was one mile behind the Boeing 747. When the radar operator saw this, he radioed Air Force One. "Air Force One, you have a bogie on your tail at one mile. Descend rapidly and be prepared to land. That bogie is out to ram you."

Air Force One started a dive and descended rapidly, but Abdul was closing fast. When the 747 was at fifteen thousand feet, Abdul had it on missile lock. He lifted the cover on a toggle switch and moved it down, and a red light came on under the arming switch that read, "Missile armed." He reached for the firing switch and moved it. The missile was activated and fired from under the wing of the Citation jet. It left with a roar, seeking the heat of the 747's jet engines.

One of the pilots of the F-16s, who were at eight thousand feet and climbing, saw the missile leave the Citation and shouted into his mike, "tower, the jet has fired a missle at air force one!" He followed the smoke trail of the missile and shouted into his mike, "air force one, you have an incoming missle. take evasive action!"

Colonel Elkhart heard the F-16 pilot and immediately banked the 747 to the left. He did not release the missile countermeasures; he had no time. The people standing in the aisles of the Boeing were thrown to the floor, and many who were not wearing seat belts fell out of their seats. The Boeing 747 was not as agile as a small jet and took a while to turn. Abdul watched as the missile streaked toward the 747 as it maneuvered to avoid the missile. But the missile found its mark. It hit the 747 in one of the jet engines and exploded, igniting the fuel tanks in the wing. It blew the 747 up in a horrendous red-and-orange fireball, sending a large boom across the sky and landscape that was seen and heard for miles. All on board were killed instantly, and the remaining parts of the 747 fell in a fireball to earth, leaving a trail of black smoke. When it hit the earth, it fell in a cornfield, exploded, and burned.

Abdul was elated when the missile hit. He smiled broadly, gave his pilot a high five, and said, "Let's get out of here and go to Canada. Head three hundred and twenty degrees." The pilot turned the Citation to a heading of three hundred and twenty degrees and pushed the throttles to full. Abdul then told him to drop down to one thousand feet.

The pilots in the F-16s were horrified as they watched Air Force One explode. The lead pilot said to the tower, "Good God Almighty! They blew up Air Force One!"

The radar operator saw the Boeing 747 disappear from his radar screen. "Sir, the F-16 pilot reports Air Force One was hit with a missile and is down, and it's gone from my screen. What do you want me to do?"

"Nothing. I'll get helicopters out to look at the crash site. When they get in the air, give them the coordinates."

He called and got the helicopters in the air. Then he phoned NORAD and talked to General Stark. "General, this is Colonel Baxter at Wright Patterson. I have bad news. A private jet equipped with a missile took down Air Force One as it was approaching Wright Patterson."

"Are you sure it was Air Force One?"

"Yes, sir. It was on approach when the private jet attacked."

"God Almighty! I suppose the president was on board."

"Yes, sir. I understand he was going to Detroit."

"What about the private jet?"

"According to our radar, he's heading for Canada."

"Are there any of our jets in the air?" General Stark asked.

"Yes, sir. Two F-16s."

"Have them take down the private jet before he gets to Canada."

"You mean shoot the jet out of the sky?"

"Of course, you idiot. Do you want the men who killed our president to get away? If they get into Canada, we will lose them. Have the fighters shoot them down, and report back to me when they do."

"Yes, Sir!" Colonel Baxter said.

He then radioed the two jets. "Arrow flight, this is Colonel Baxter. Your orders are to catch the private jet that fired on Air Force One and take him down. Is that clear?"

"Yes, sir! Fire on the private jet with our missiles and take him down. Roger."

The lead pilot changed radio frequencies and said to the other jet pilot, "You heard the man. Let's go. Turn on your afterburners."

The jets, with their afterburners on, reached Mach 1.2 and, in a short time, caught up to the Citation jet. Abdul had passed Detroit and was over Lake Huron at one hundred feet over the water, traveling at maximum airspeed, five hundred and twenty-two knots. He was feeling good. He had accomplished his mission and was unaware the two fighter jets were closing in on him.

When the F-16s were within a quarter mile, the lead pilot said to the other pilot, "I have a missile locked on the jet. Do you?"

"Yes, sir."

"Okay, fire!"

Two missiles left the jets and went screaming toward the Citation. Abdul began to look at his air map and started to say to his pilot, "Pretty soon—"

He never finished what he started to say. The two missiles hit the Citation jet, blowing it up into a thousand pieces and into a red-hot orange-and-red fireball. It fell into Lake Huron and sank, leaving a debris field on top of the water as well as jet fuel. The two jets went over the debris field, verified no one survived, then turned and headed back to base.

The lead pilot radioed to Wright Patterson. "This is Arrow flight. Private jet taken out and downed in Lake Huron. No survivors. Mission accomplished."

Colonel Baxter called General Stark at NORAD. "General, the private jet that took down Air Force One is down in Lake Huron. Our fighters took him out."

"Very well. Did anyone get a tail number on that jet?"

"Yes, sir. The lead pilot did."

"Okay, track it and call me back when you identify the owner."

"Yes, sir!"

General Stark called the pentagon and talked to the chief of staff, General Berger. He told him about Air Force One, the shooting down of the private jet, and the death of the president. When he hung up, General Berger realized that the country had no president and would have no one in authority in case of an emergency. So he called the White House and talked to Paul Barrows.

He said, "Paul, this is General Berger. I have some shocking and sad news. Is the vice president around?"

"No, sir. She's at a hospital with her sick grandchild."

"Well, get her to the White House at once. And make sure she has plenty of Secret Service protection."

"Okay, I can do that. What's the shocking news?"

"The president is dead!"

"*What?* Gerald Harrison dead? How?"

"Air Force One was shot down with a missile from a private jet going into Wright Paterson. All on board are dead."

"Good God! Yes, I see your point. We don't have a president. I'll get Grace Arden over here right away. Has this news been released to the public?"

"No. Maybe Grace would want to do that."

"Yes. I'll ask her," Paul said.

As soon as he hung up, he went to the office of Timothy Hendricks. He didn't knock on Hendricks's door; he just burst into his office. Hendricks was sitting, reading a paper. He looked up, surprised. "Paul, what's wrong? Your face is white."

"Tim, the president is dead."

"Dead! How? Where?"

"Air Force One was shot down with a missile going into Wright Patterson. Everyone on board is dead."

"Are you sure? Has this been confirmed?"

"General Berger, the chief of staff, just called me. We'd better get more protection for Grace. She could be next. Remember the Eagle Down plot?"

"You're right. Where is she?"

"At General Hospital with her daughter, looking after her granddaughter."

"Okay. I'll send additional men over there and bring her back."

"Don't tell her why, Tim. Just tell her it's an emergency. I'll tell her when she gets here."

"You'd better alert the chief justice. He should come over and swear her in."

"You're right. I'll do that right away."

An hour and a half later, Grace came into Paul's office and sat down. "What's the big deal, Paul? I was hustled out of the hospital room. The agent said it was urgent, and I never had such a large police escort before. What gives?"

"Grace, this is difficult for me—"

"Paul, what's wrong? You have tears in your eyes."

"Grace . . . Gerald Harrison . . . is dead!"

"Oh my god! How? Where? When?"

"We believe the Ghost, in a Citation jet outfitted with a missile, shot down Air Force One near Dayton, Ohio, just as the plane was descending to land. Everyone on board was killed. I'm sorry, so sorry, to have to tell you this. You know what that means, don't you?"

"Yes! I am the new president!"

"Exactly. I thought it best if the chief justice came over and swore you in immediately in a private ceremony. If you want a public ceremony later, we can arrange that. What do you think, Madam President?"

"Paul, I'm not the president yet."

"I know. I was just practicing."

"Paul, that's fine. This is just a shock. I don't know what to do or say, for that matter."

"Don't worry. Things will come up that you have to decide on pretty quick. You'll get the hang of it."

Just then, Samuel Richards, the chief justice of the Supreme Court, walked into Paul's office. "Hello, Paul and Grace. I came as soon as I got your message, Paul. You said it was very urgent."

"Yes, now hold on to yourself, Mr. Justice, for what I have to tell you."

"Is it bad news?"

"Yes, sir! The president, Gerald Harrison, is dead. He was assassinated this morning aboard Air Force One."

"Did someone shoot him?"

"No. A plane shot a missile at Air Force One and shot it down. Everyone on board was killed."

"My god! How awful. Oh, now I get it. You want me to swear in Grace as the president."

"Exactly."

"Fine, I can do that. We should have witnesses."

"Fine, let's do the swearing in the press room. I'll get the whole White House staff there. Grace—excuse me, Madam President—will you show the chief justice to the pressroom? I'll have my secretary bring the Bible from the oval office there. I'll round up the staff, and when we get them in the room, I'll make an announcement about the president.

When all the White House staff was in the pressroom, Paul got up behind the lectern, cleared his throat, and said, "Ladies and gentlemen, I have very sad news today. Gerald Harrison, our beloved president, was assassinated this morning. I cannot go into any more details than that. In a short time, I will announce to the press the whole story of the assassination. The business at hand now is to swear in our new president so our government can function. I have asked you here as witnesses to the swearing-in ceremony. We will have a formal swearing-in at a later time. Thank you. Now, Mr. Chief Justice, will you administer the oath of office?"

After Grace Arden took the oath of office, she asked Paul to announce the president's death to the press. Paul asked the press secretary to call the press corps into the pressroom. When the press was seated, Paul walked up to the lectern. This raised immediate questions in the minds of the press since the press secretary usually made announcements.

"Ladies and gentlemen, I have some very sad news for you and for the people of the United States," Paul said. "This morning, Air Force One was carrying the president, some press representatives, and a number of advisers to Detroit for a rally the president was giving to gain support for his stimulus bill. As the plane was approaching for a landing at Wright Patterson Air Force base, a civilian jet, a Citation X armed with a missile, shot down the plane. Everyone on board was killed—"

Before he could continue, the room was abuzz with conversations.

"Ladies and gentlemen, please, please let me finish."

The room quieted down, and Paul went on.

"We don't have much more information except that two F-16 fighter jets from Wright Patterson shot down the Citation. We believe the assassin was a killer from the Middle East known by Interpol as the Ghost. We don't know who is behind the plot, but we believe president Harrison was murdered to keep his stimulus bill from becoming law. All federal law enforcement is working on the case. That's all I have on the tragedy. A little while ago, Grace Arden, the vice president, was sworn in as president of the United States by the chief justice. This ceremony was witnessed by the White House staff. As more information becomes available, the press secretary will keep you posted. Thank you."

Paul left the podium as the whole room burst into conversations and questions, while some ran to get the news to their TV stations and newspapers.

When Paul got back to his office, he phoned Clive Banner. When Clive heard the news, he called his entire staff and agents together. Standing in front of them, he said, "Ladies and gentlemen, I have just received some very bad and very sad news. Our president, Gerald Harrison, has been assassinated. Air Force One was shot down by a missile from a private jet, killing all on board. Our F-16s shot down the private jet. Grace Arden has been sworn in as our new president. That's all I have for now. The whole story will be on the news right away. Dan Morris, will you come to my office?"

When Dan sat down in Clive's office, Clive was still emotional from hearing the news. "Bear with me, Dan. I knew and liked this man. I feel very sad about his death."

"That's okay, Chief. Take your time."

He paused for a moment then said, "Hassan is the only link we have to the men behind this plot. What do you think it will take to get him to reveal his partners?"

"I don't know, Chief. When I interrogated him, he was adamant about keeping his mouth shut."

"We can't set him free, but suppose the justice department offered him no death penalty? Just life in prison?"

"No parole, ever?"

"Yeah, do you think he would go for that?"

"I don't know. I doubt it. He's a coldblooded killer. He knew the risks when he went into his profession. Maybe if he saw some light at the end of the tunnel, like parole after thirty-five or twenty-five years, he might go for it. I'm not a practicing lawyer and haven't dealt with sentencing, so I really don't have a feel for what condemned men settle for."

"Okay, Dan, I just wanted to see if you had a feel for this man."

"By the way, can I tell Carol from the *Washington Ledger* they can print the whole story about Eagle Down?"

"Sure, why not? The secret is out. Only the details are unknown. Go ahead. Give her the go-ahead."

When Dan gave Carol the go-ahead, she and Bob went into Sam's office and laid out the story they would write. Sam's last comment was "Get all the facts, and fast. I want to put out an extra before the other papers beat us to it."

* * *

That evening, Grace went on all the TV networks and told the public about the tragedy.

"Good evening, my countrymen. It is with a heavy heart that I speak with you tonight as your new president. Our president, Gerald Harrison, has been assassinated by a lone assassin who shot Air Force One out of the sky. The nation is mourning his loss. At this time, we know who committed this despicable act, a hired killer from the Far East known only as the Ghost, but we don't know who hired him. But let me assure you that all the law enforcement forces of the United States government will be used to root out the culprits and bring them to justice for this heinous crime. But for the grace of God, I was supposed to join Gerald Harrison on that trip to Detroit, but another matter came up that I had to attend to. My grandchild was ill in the hospital. Ever since his inauguration, I have worked closely with President Harrison in forming his plans to get this country out of the recession and get us back to a financial recovery by putting our unemployed back to work, helping small businesses to expand, and getting our factories' output up to their potential. He planned to do this with his bill known as the stimulus bill. For months now, that bill has been stalled in Congress and debated and debated. It is time to end the debate and get this bill to a vote in the House and Senate. I ask all citizens to e-mail, call, or write their senators and representatives to bring this bill to a vote and move this country to where our late president wanted to take us. As your president, I know where President Harrison wanted to go, and I pledge I will follow the road he has laid out. Plans for a memorial for our late president are being formed and will be announced tomorrow. Thank you, and may God bless America. Good night."

Clive realized he was at a brick wall. He suspected Saxton and Giddings to be behind the plot but had no evidence to support his suspicions. He decided to put a meeting together with the president, Grace Arden, the CIA, Interpol, and the Secret Service. He called Paul Barrows and set it up. When they were all in the oval office, Paul said to Clive, "Mr. Banner, you called the meeting. What did you want to discuss?"

"Finding the man or men behind the plot to kill the president."

"Did you have something in mind?" asked Grace.

"Yes. First, let me say we have evidence that this man, Hassan, is the killer of four people to keep the plot under wraps. We know he planted the bomb in the garage of our building. Why? I can only guess. We were getting close to uncovering the plot, and either he or his fellow conspirators decided to plant a bomb to occupy us with finding the bomber and take our resources off the Eagle Down plot. The Ghost is dead, so the only link we have to the planners of this plot is Hassan. We feel he was in contact with the Ghost and acted as the go-between with the Ghost and the perpetrators of the plot. Now, what I have to propose may seem distasteful, but I believe it's the only chance we have of finding these men."

"What do you propose, Mr. Banner?" asked Grace.

"The crimes this man has committed unquestionably warrant the death penalty. But if we sentence and kill him, his secret goes to the grave with him. So offer him a life sentence with a chance of parole in twenty-five years."

"Parole in twenty-five years? After murdering four people, being complicit in killing the president, and blowing up a building and injuring over forty people? That's a cakewalk for him," said Timothy Hendricks.

"I know. That's why I said it might be distasteful. But if we don't get him to come clean, we may never find the men responsible for assassinating the president. What do you think, Madam President?"

"You have no leads, Clive?"

"No, Ma'am. We have a recording of Saxton talking to a man on the morning the building was blown up and saying that the day had arrived and 'Don't kill anyone.' We think they were talking about the bombing of the building but can't prove it. The woman who had a copy of the plan worked in Saxton's office. So did his aide, Jerry Baldwin. Everything points to him, but we have no proof."

"Then I guess we don't have an alternative," Grace said. "I want the men that killed our president. And if those men are the leaders in the House and Senate, I don't want this country to be led by murderers, even if it means giving a light sentence to a mass murderer. Do you think he will accept that sentence for his testimony?"

"I don't know. I suggest we get ahold of his attorney, Austin McGregor, and the federal prosecutor, Ron Carter, and propose it to them and let them take it to Hassan Kahil."

"All right, Clive. Go ahead and pray he takes the offer, as abhorrent as it seems," replied Grace.

* * *

Clive called Ron Carter and told him what the president had decided on.

"Yes, Mr. Banner. My boss, the attorney general, told me what the president had decided and told me to go ahead with the offer. I called Austin McGregor, and we planned on meeting this afternoon with Hassan. Do you want to be there?"

"No, but I'd like Dan Morris there. He's been heading up the investigation. I'll give him a call and have him meet you there."

"Fine. Say, four o'clock?"

* * *

At four o'clock, a guard brought Hassan into an interrogation room. He was handcuffed and had leg irons on his ankles. As he walked in, he was surprised to see the prosecutor. "Sit down, Hassan," McGregor said. "These gentlemen have an offer for you."

Hassan sat down and looked at both Dan and Ron with a quizzical expression on his face. Ron started the conversation. "Mr. Kahil, as I told you before, we have an airtight case against you for the murder of four people, the bombing of the FBI building, and now, complicity in the assassination of the president of the United States, any one of which would carry the death penalty. We know that you were the go-between to the men who planned this assassination and the killer called the Ghost. For your information, the Ghost succeeded in killing the president, but not the vice president, who is now the president."

"Did the Ghost get away?" asked Hassan.

"No. His plane was shot down by our fighter planes."

"Too bad. He was the best."

"Well, best or not, he's dead. Now, getting back to you, Mr. Kahil. We want the men who planned this plot, and you know who they are. They can't help you now. The president will nominate a new vice president, so the men who thought to gain from this plot will not change their position and will not be able to help you. Now, do you want to get a needle in your arm and pass into eternity, or would you be willing to tell us who those men are and save your skin?"

"If you are offering me life in prison, then I would prefer the needle rather than spend forty or fifty years in prison. So screw your offer."

"Okay, suppose I said you could be paroled in thirty-five years. How would that sit with you?"

"Thirty-five years? That's like a life sentence. Forget it."

"Mr. Kahil, you realize you have committed some heinous crimes. I don't know how the public would feel if we let you off too easily."

"That's your problem. If you let me out in fifteen years, I'll roll on my employers."

"No, Mr. Kahil, I can't do that. But I'll tell you what. You give us the names of those men and help us get some evidence against them, and I'll go for twenty-five to life, which makes you eligible for parole in twenty-five years."

"How can I get evidence on them if I'm in jail?"

"Don't worry about that. We can use the phone and record your conversation."

"What do you think, Mr. McGregor?" asked Hassan. "Mr. Kahil, they have a solid case against you, and I'm sure they will get a conviction. The offer is a generous one. I advise you to take it," replied McGregor.

"Okay, as you Americans say, you got a deal."

"I brought a recorder with me. I want you to tell me everything, and I will record it. Mr. Morris here will quiz you."

"Okay, what do you want to know?"

"First, who is behind this plot? Who hired you?" asked Dan.

"Senator Saxton and that man Giddings."

"House Speaker Samuel Giddings?"

"Yes."

"What did they want you to do?"

"Get in touch with the best assassin in Europe and hire him to kill the president and vice president."

"Who told them about the Ghost?"

"I did."

"Who told you to murder the Bigelows and those other people?"

"Senator Saxton."

"Why were they killed?"

"Saxton had his aide Baldwin in on the plot. He was promised a high position in the government when Giddings and Saxton were made president and vice president. But he screwed up and let a woman in Saxton's office get ahold of the plan. He gave it to her and had her deliver it to Giddings. But he failed to seal the envelope. She opened it and read it then copied it. Saxton had the phones in his office tapped, so he found out she had a copy when she phoned a reporter with the paper. When Bigelow sent the e-mail to Saxton, he ordered me to take him out and his wife in case he had said something to her. No one was to know about the plan."

"So he ordered you to kill all four?"

"Yes, on the phone. I have only met Saxton twice, once when he hired me and once when he wanted me to blow up the FBI garage. All other instructions were on the phone."

"Did Saxton use a cell phone?"

"Yes, all the time."

"Why did he want his aide murdered?"

"He saw the reporters talking to him a lot and even saw them go to his house, and he was afraid Baldwin would talk to the reporters. Besides, he had no further need of him. He used him to type the plan into his computer."

"Is the plan still in his computer?"

"I don't know."

"You ran the reporters off the road. Why did you try to kill them?"

"I didn't try to kill them, just take them out of circulation until the president was dead. They were asking too many questions and talking to too many people, and Saxton wanted to silence them. But he said not to kill them."

"How did the Ghost know when the president would be in Detroit?"

"Saxton got his trip schedule and e-mailed it to me, and I gave it to Abdul Basara, the Ghost."

"The Ghost? That was his name? Abdul Basara?"

"Yes, he lived in Cairo. I went there to hire him."

"Was he in Washington?"

"Yes. That was when I gave him the president's schedule."

"How was the Ghost paid?"

"He got two and a half million to start. The money was wired to his Swiss bank account. I have the number in my wallet."

"Who wired the money?"

"I don't know. I just gave the account number and bank name to Saxton."

"Anything else, Mr. Kahil?"   I

"No, that's about it. Now what happens? When I talked to Saxton after I was arrested, he said when he got to be vice president and Giddings was president, they would pardon me and I could leave the country."

"Well, they are not getting those positions, and you are not getting out of jail. As for the next move, just sit tight. I'll get back to you," said Ron.

CHAPTER 9

Clive took the recording to the oval office and played it for Grace Arden and Paul. When it was through, they sat in silence for a bit. Then Grace said, "I can't believe that two men in the highest positions in our government could be so wicked or evil. Are you going to arrest them, Clive?"

"No. We want more evidence to corroborate with Hassan's story."

"How do you plan on getting that?"

"We plan on Hassan calling from jail and asking Saxton to help him get out of jail. Of course, Saxton has no power to help him, but we will coach Hassan to get Saxton to incriminate himself about giving Hassan orders."

"Then?"

"We arrest him and Giddings and get a search warrant for their office, computer, house, and telephone records. If we get lucky, Saxton may not have deleted the plan from his computer. But with this recording, Hassan's testimony, and whatever we find in our search warrant, we have enough to convict them."

"Clive, have you found out who this Ghost was?"

"Yes. One of the F-16 pilots copied the tail number off the Citation jet. The FAA traced it to a leasing company in Saudi Arabia that leased it to Abdul Basara, who lived in Cairo. Hassan has verified that was his name. We gave that information to Interpol. They have been after him for a number of years. That will clear up a number of cases for them."

"Where did the money used to pay that enormous sum to the Ghost come from?" the new president asked.

"As of yet, we don't know. Hassan gave us his bank and bank account number in Switzerland. We are working with the Swiss government to give us that information. If we knew the account number and bank that the money was transferred from, we could find out who supplied the funds and whether they are involved."

"Okay, Clive. Let me know when you are going to arrest Saxton and Giddings. When you do, the Senate and House will have to elect a new majority leader for the Senate and a new speaker for the House. Then maybe we can get a vote on the stimulus bill," Graced finished.

* * *

The nation was mourning for their dead president. There were thousands of e-mails coming into the White House expressing condolences, and they overwhelmed the computers. Outside the White House, people were bringing flowers and bouquets and leaving them at the fence with a note. Some lit candles and left them. Others left notes and cards on the fence. Letters and notes from foreign dignitaries all over the world were pouring in. When Air Force One crashed, it burned up everything. No bodies or recognizable parts of the aircraft were left. The people had no flag-draped coffin to pass by and pay their respects to. This void hurt.

Grace sat with some of her staff to figure out a way for the country to pay their respects. In the long run, only a memorial service and some kind of monument that people could observe would suffice. They decided to hold a memorial service and broadcast it over all the networks. They also decided to have a six-foot marble cross sculpture and a bronze plaque made with a bronze casting of Harrison's face placed on the sculpture. It had "Gerald Harrison, President of the United States" on it and the dates of his birth and death, and it was placed in Arlington Cemetery, near the John F. Kennedy burial plot, where people could come and pay their respects.

* * *

Don Carter and Dan met with Hassan, and they coached him on what to say to Saxton on the phone and how to get him to admit how he asked Hassan to murder people and get the Ghost to join the plot. When he was ready, Hassan called Saxton from a phone with a recorder to record the conversation.

Saxton answered his phone. "Yes?"

"This is Hassan, Mr. Saxton."

"Don't use my name on the phone. Someone could be listening."

"I see we have a new president and it isn't you or Mr. Giddings."

"No."

"The last time we talked, you said as soon as you and Mr. Giddings were in the White House, you would get me a pardon. So what happens now?"

"We will have to hire someone to kill the new president."

Don Carter was listening with earphones to the conversation. When Saxton said he would hire someone to kill Grace, he smiled broadly. Saxton was incriminating himself.

"And how long will that take?"

"I don't know. I have to find someone first."

"Do you think you will find someone like the Ghost?"

"Yes," Saxton said, appearing to be confident.

"In the meantime, I sit in jail, waiting to be tried for murders you told me to commit."

"Be patient, Hassan. I will get you out. Just keep your mouth shut."

"When you told me to kill the Bigelows, that Manning woman, and your aide, Jerry Baldwin, you said I wouldn't be caught if I carried out your instructions."

"Look, I told you to kill those people, but not how, and it was up to you to carry out the murders so you wouldn't be caught. Remember, I told you to get rid of the gun and dump it in the Potomac River. You didn't. I can't help it if you don't carry out all my instructions."

"What about the FBI building? You said blow it up but don't kill anyone. I did that, and no one died."

"Yes, that was handled right."

"Tell me, why did you want to blow up that building?"

"I told you, to get the FBI to look for the bomber and to quit looking for us, the people behind the plot to kill the president. Why are you asking all these questions?"

"Because I don't like being in jail, and I want out."

"Hassan, you were well paid for your services. You said you were a professional and took the risks. Yes, I planned all those crimes, but you carried them out and got caught. So quit complaining and sit tight. It will take time, but we will get you out."

Saxton hung up. Hassan turned and looked at Don, who had a wide grin on his face. "Perfect," he said to Hassan. "That man just hung himself."

"That wraps it up for us," said Dan.

Dan and Don took the recording to Clive Banner and played it for him. When Clive heard it, he said, "Now, Don, I suppose you want me to arrest them both?"

"Yes. And I will get search warrants from the judge. Then you can conduct your search."

* * *

Senator Saxton was in the Senate, sitting, listening to a senator speaking. Dan and another FBI agent and two policemen walked in and went to his seat. Saxton, surprised at their presence, looked up at the men. Dan said, "Senator Saxton, please stand up."

"What is this?" replied Saxton.

"Senator, please stand up. You are under arrest for the murder of four people and for planning the assassination of the president."

"This is preposterous!" said Saxton out loud. All the men in the Senate heard Saxton and looked at Saxton in surprise.

Dan reached down, grabbed Saxton by the arm, and pulled him up by the arm. He turned him around and handcuffed him, read him his rights, and took him out to a police cruiser. A short time later, Giddings was arrested in the House of Representatives.

* * *

Dan Morris called Carol and gave her the story. Again, an extra was on the street with the story of the two men being arrested. People in Washington were stunned as they read the paper. The TV broadcasts were filled with the story. The population was shocked that two of the highest politicians in the country were guilty of such heinous crimes.

Clive went to the lockup and had Saxton and Giddings brought to an interrogation room. They sat down across him at a table. Saxton was the first to speak. "Clive, get us out of here. This is preposterous, arresting the two top men in the government."

"I can't do that, George. You and Sam here are going to be charged with four counts of conspiracy to commit murder, conspiracy to assassinate the president of the United States, and blowing up the garage of the FBI building. You both have seen your last day as free men."

"But you have no evidence linking us to those crimes!"

"Oh yes, we have. First, you should be more careful when you talk on the phone. You convicted yourself when you spoke with Hassan yesterday. Also, Hassan has agreed to testify against you, and his testimony is very damaging. This morning, we searched your office and found the Eagle Down plot on your computer. And, George, it had a date long before any of the crimes were committed. Also, we found the e-mail on your computer where you sent the president's schedule to Hassan. Yes, we have enough evidence to put you two away for life," Clive said.

* * *

In less than a week, George Saxton and Samuel Giddings were indicted by a federal grand jury on four counts of conspiracy to commit murder and one count of conspiracy to assassinate the president of the United States. They were also charged with conspiracy to bomb the FBI building. Conspiracy charges do not carry a death penalty, but both men would spend the rest of their lives in jail.

Hassan pleaded guilty to the four murders, assisting in the plot to kill the president, and setting off a bomb in the FBI building and was sentenced to twenty-five years to life for his part in the plot. He would be eligible for parole in twenty-five years.

The Swiss government held fast to their policy of keeping bank records secret, so the FBI never found out where the money that was paid to Abdul the Ghost came from. Clive felt it could have come from some rich industrialist or the party's national committee and there could have been other men in on the plot, but at the least, he had found and convicted the three main characters involved in the plot.

Carol and Bob received a Pulitzer Prize for their investigation and reporting of the Eagle Down plot. Carol soon had her own byline on the paper; she was now a full-fledged newspaper reporter, achieving her dreams.

Grace Arden went before a joint session of Congress and gave a speech imploring the Congress to pass the stimulus bill in memory of Gerald Harrison's vision of bringing the country out of the deep recession and pledged to follow his plans for the country. When the vote was taken a week later, the House passed the bill with a majority of two hundred and sixty for the bill and one hundred and seventy-two against. The Senate voted overwhelmingly eighty for and twenty against. Grace was elected for a second term. She was a very popular president.

Time would determine if Gerald Harrison's vision was correct and would bring the country back to full employment and a robust economy.

The End

ABOUT THE AUTHOR

I am a writer, and I became a writer late in life, when I was eighty years old. I found I thoroughly enjoy writing stories, creating characters and situations. I began by writing my biography so my children would know who their father was and what his life was about when I was gone from this beautiful blue planet. I found that I could write reasonably good stories, and I enjoyed it, so I began with a story I called "The Poet—a Tale of a Serial Killer." When I finished it, I sent it to my siblings to read. They thought it was quite good, which only encouraged me to write more. My next effort was a western, a story of two young men who went through the Civil War and decided to go west and see the country. This was my first attempt to get a book published. I called it *Two Rode West*.

Ron Marr did the professional editing of that book, as all books have to be professionally edited before the publisher will accept them for publication. He has written a number of books and is an editor of a western paper in the western states and is considered a well-known author. He complimented me on the book and said he enjoyed reading and editing my work. This only encouraged me to go on.

Since then I have written twenty-three novels and have had eight published, three by Eloquent Books and five by PublishAmerica.

I was never a good student in school; I was a daydreamer as a youngster in grammar school. As a youngster, I had a talent for drawing and begged my father to send me to art school, but he refused. I wanted a life of art, not academics. It was in the spring of 1945 when I joined the marine corps that my life really began. The war ended before I saw any action in battles. The farthest I got was Pearl Harbor. After the war, I attended Rutgers University, but that was interrupted by my moving to California. I found a job with a food company called Hunt Foods. I stayed with that firm for thirty-seven years, working as an accountant then a controller. I retired in 1985 and worked as a consultant for five years. Then I started to learn to parachute, which led to taking flying lessons. I loved the wild blue yonder. I received my private pilot's license in 1995 at age 69. I flew for twelve years before a medical condition caused me stop flying. It was then I started writing.

My books are all fiction and vary as far as topics are concerned. I have written four westerns, three stories of the military: one about submarines in the Pacific during World War II, another about men aboard an aircraft carrier in World War II, and a third about a pilot in World War II that starts his own airline. In addition, I wrote five murder novels, three adventure stories, and a political thriller and have finished two more stories, another western about men crossing the country in the 1820s, like Lewis and Clark, and a story of terrorists bombing American icons in New York City, a story of an young Italian young man who comes to America to own and captain his own boat, and, finally, a story of a small-town lawyer in the South during the Great Depression in 1938. Then I wrote a story about four boys who camp out on the shore of a lake in Oregon and get into trouble and help capture two bank robbers. They learn to sail a boat and get into races on the lake.

My novels are not long, usually a little more than two hundred pages, so one can get through them in several days. Take a chance and buy one, and I promise you hours of reading pleasure. The narrative below describes the novels that have been published and the ones that maybe I might get published.

CPSIA information can be obtained
at www.ICGtesting.com
Printed in the USA
LVHW050559040523
745964LV00002B/165